RETURN OF THE WITCH

RETURN OF THE WITCH

THE WITCH NEXT DOOR™ BOOK SIX

JUDITH BERENS

This book is a work of fiction.
All of the characters, organizations, and events portrayed in this novel are either products of the author's imagination or are used fictitiously. Sometimes both.

Copyright © 2019 Judith Berens, Martha Carr & Michael Anderle
Cover by Fantasy Book Design
Cover copyright © LMBPN Publishing
A Michael Anderle Production

LMBPN Publishing supports the right to free expression and the value of copyright. The purpose of copyright is to encourage writers and artists to produce the creative works that enrich our culture.

The distribution of this book without permission is a theft of the author's intellectual property. If you would like permission to use material from the book (other than for review purposes), please contact support@lmbpn.com. Thank you for your support of the author's rights.

LMBPN Publishing
PMB 196, 2540 South Maryland Pkwy
Las Vegas, NV 89109

First US edition, November 2019
Version 1.01, December 2020
ebook ISBN: 978-1-64202-586-6
Print ISBN: 978-1-64202-587-3

Thanks to the JIT Readers

Jeff Eaton
Dorothy Lloyd
Diane L. Smith
Larry Omans

If we've missed anyone, please let us know!

Editor
SkyHunter Editing Team

From Martha

To everyone who still believes in magic
and all the possibilities that holds.
To all the readers who make this
entire ride so much fun.
And to my son, Louie and so many wonderful friends who
remind me all the time of what
really matters and how wonderful
life can be in any given moment.

From Michael

To Family, Friends and
Those Who Love
To Read.
May We All Enjoy Grace
To Live The Life We Are
Called.

ONE

O n the west coast of a Grecian peninsula a few miles outside Savalia, Lily Antony stared at the glistening Mediterranean Sea and pressed Romeo's cellphone to her ear. "But after all that, Bentley, I promise, we're fine."

Her mom's accountant and long-time friend, Bentley McClure, released a heavy sigh on the other end of the line. "You're exactly like your mother, Lily. I know you can take care of yourself, the same way she always managed to power her way through anything and everything that tried to stop her. That doesn't mean I don't still worry about you. Especially when our last phone call ended with an explosion and considerable shouting."

Lily scuffed her bare foot across the white sands of the beach where she and Romeo had parked her 2002 Winnebago Adventurer—a gift from Bentley before she'd had to flee Charleston and head off in search of her mom. "I know. I'm sorry it took me a few days to get back to you."

He snorted. "It's better than not hearing from you for six months while the rest of the world thinks you're dead."

"Well, I have something to help against these people that my mom never had."

"What might that be?"

She grinned. "I have a werewolf traveling with me, numerous visions in my back pocket, and an insanely powerful witch feeding me information from the inside."

His chuckle was a little dry and strained. "Indeed. If Greta Antony had Greta Antony to help her, I imagine she wouldn't have found herself nearly as entangled in this mess."

"Well, now she has me." The side door to the Winnie banged shut behind her, and Lily turned away from the beach. A shirtless Romeo stood outside the RV, stretched his arms up above his head, and indulged a growl of satisfaction. The sun rising behind the vehicle was a perfectly golden backlight to her werewolf friend who'd become so much more than only a friend. Before she let herself get too distracted by the sight, she turned away and gazed at the lightening sky. "I hate having to ask a favor, and maybe it's a little redundant, seeing as we're all the way out here—"

"Anything, Lily."

"Would you mind putting money in my bank account? Not to use while we're here. My phone was disconnected, and that's how I realized things are a little empty in the bank. I'd like to have a phone just in case."

"That's your favor?" Bentley sounded like he was trying not to laugh.

"Only this one payment. We're so close, Bentley. We almost found her. And I can repay you as soon as we get back to the States. Seriously, I still have a few giant bags of gold coins—"

This time, the man she'd known her whole life as the stoic, proper, immaculately precise man with an incredible amount of love for Greta Antony and her daughter burst out laughing. "Lily, if you bring her home again in one piece—if you come home in one piece—I'll pay your phone bill for an entire year."

Lily wrinkled her nose. "Well, that won't be necessary."

"Of course I can help you with that, Lily. I'll send the funds over as soon as I'm off the phone with you."

"Thank you." She sighed gratefully and buried her toes in the sand. "I never quite got to tell you the rest of the important stuff the last time I called. Grab a pen and write down this number." When the man gave her the go-ahead, she glanced at the magical business card in her other hand. The words scrolled across in navy-blue letters and gold flashes of light and she read the number out.

"Who does this belong to?" Bentley asked.

"A man named Gabriel Mercier." Lily flipped the card over and nodded at the crest of the magical Order whose members were spread across Europe. "He's a detective with Non-Magical Relations for Cadre Europa."

"I see."

"And before you try to ask in a subtly skeptical way, no, I did not get into any trouble with an Order out here."

He chuckled. "It never crossed my mind."

"We met Gabriel in France, and he told us enough to make it perfectly clear that the Council and most of the magical world has no idea what the Black Heron's up to. Hopefully, when you call him, you guys can start changing that." She cleared her throat and recalled one more man she'd connected with the French witch detective. "Do you know anyone in Romania named Darius?"

"Lily, I don't know anyone in Romania, period."

"Fair enough. Gabriel should have gotten in touch with Darius. I hope. The man's a healer and has a ton of information about the Black Heron. He was putting it all together with Mom right before they took her."

There was a long pause, and Bentley took a deep breath. "Then I suppose the man is worth reaching out to as well. Does he have a last name?"

"I...actually, we never quite got that far. The minute he told me he knew my mom, I kinda forgot to ask."

"That's fine, Lily. I'll call this detective, and I'm sure he'll be able to fill me in on the rest. It gives me an opportunity to brush up on my French, anyway."

Lily smirked. "Remind me to show you this little spell I put together for language translation."

"I'll put it on the list of things to cover when you, Romeo, and your mother are safely back where you belong."

"Good. Thanks for everything, Bentley. I wish I could say I'll call you soon, but I'm not exactly sure what'll happen from here on out."

"Well, at least I'll know it's a call from your own phone

the next time I hear from you. You be safe, Lily. And bring her home."

"That's exactly what I plan to do. Bye, Bentley." She ended the call, turned the screen off on Romeo's phone, and stared at the glittering blue waves that seemed to stretch for endless miles. *The sea is the sea. It smells like home. At least there's something familiar here.*

Two hands settled on her waist, and she tilted her head enough for Romeo to hook his chin over her shoulder as he wound his arms around her. "How'd the call go?"

She leaned back against him and settled into the warmth of her one constant comfort since she'd left South Carolina a little over two months before. "Well, it wasn't interrupted by Black Heron magicals and their experiments gone wrong. There were no explosions and no crazy magic. So it was a good conversation."

He chuckled and kissed her cheek. "Did you give him that detective's number?"

"Yep." She turned away from him a little to meet his gaze and raised an eyebrow. "Have you had any luck on finding us a freighter going that way?" She lifted a finger to point across the Mediterranean in the general direction of their next destination—Libya.

"There are numerous freighters, Lil. That's not the problem."

When he didn't say anything else, she laughed and turned in his arms to face him. "You can't simply say there's a problem and leave it at that."

"Yeah, I know. I looked into every one of them. They have all kinds of hoops to go through in order to get us on one of those giant boats. The ones that are big enough for the Winnie are commercial only, and there's a crapload of paperwork that goes with it."

"That's really not gonna help us."

"No kidding."

Standing on her tiptoes, Lily left a quick kiss on his lips before she slipped out of his arms. "It sounds like we'd better get a move on, then. How far away is the closest?"

"About an hour and a half." Romeo smirked and watched her dance her way across the beach toward their house on wheels.

"That's a ridiculously short drive after all the stretches we've done."

"Yeah, but I have a feeling we'll only be turned away by every single shipyard we come across. They want us to fill out papers and a manifest, and then there are customs. Not to mention the fact that most people prefer to be paid with credit cards or actual money."

"Was that specifically stated in their terms? 'Sorry, we don't take solid-gold coins.'" She grinned cheekily at him as she opened the Winnie's side door and waited for him to catch up.

"No. It wasn't specifically stated anywhere."

"Hey, we managed to wiggle our way onto the *Atlantic Maiden* from South America to France with gold coins and a little magical bartering. And I doubt Captain Kruzjic had a contingency plan for that." She offered him his cell phone, and he took it with a smirk before he followed her inside the RV.

"We had a tip about Kruzjic potentially being willing

to take us across the ocean under the table. Unfortunately, we don't know anyone here who could point us in the right direction."

Lily clambered into the passenger seat and stared out the window at the sea. "You know, if I'd known it was safe to go back to Otiylo, we could've asked Ozias."

"It's not safe."

"I know that." She waited until he joined her in the front and slid into the driver's seat, his expression attentive. "If we go back there it's more dangerous for us than it is for them. I'm not gonna bring the Black Heron down on those people's heads again. They already did too much to help us."

"I think that's a fairly good call."

With a nod, she gestured toward the wide, tall wind-shield. "Let's get moving up the coast, then. We obviously don't have any problems making friends and asking around for magical deals to get this thing across the water."

Romeo chuckled and started the engine. "You make it sound so easy."

"It is easy."

"Except for the fact that I can't plan any of this before we simply start approaching random strangers to ask if they'll take our gold for a secret trip across the Mediter-ranean Sea with no paper trail."

"Hustling for under-the-table deals is an art form, Romeo." She winked at him and buckled her seatbelt. "Consider all this good practice."

He laughed, shifted into drive, and eased the vehicle

across the sand toward the main road. "Oh, yeah? Does that mean you've had practice with hustling?"

"I might have." She leaned back in the seat and stretched her legs out in front of her.

"I'm not sure that hustling in high school to get into clubs with a fake ID is on the same level as making a secret deal with a legit cargo freighter to take us to Libya."

"Oh, come on, Romeo." Lily grinned and gave him a playful punch in the arm. "I still have a few tricks up my sleeve."

He did a double-take and squinted at her before he focused on the road again. "I'd like to think I already know all your tricks."

"Well, let's say that—watch out!"

Romeo braked sharply, and the Winnie lurched to a stop much faster than the brakes were capable of managing. In the center of Highway E09 stood a creature barely under four feet tall wearing dark, green-black pants that were frayed at the edges. It stretched its hand toward them and engulfed the RV in a blaze of green light, making the entire vehicle lurch again where it had already stopped on the road.

"Who's the frogman?" Romeo shouted.

The huge, bulging eyes on the green-skinned creature's face narrowed, and the pulsing column of green light continued to churn from its outstretched hands to keep its newest victims right where they were.

"Back up," Lily muttered.

"Yep." He threw the Winnie into reverse and floored the gas pedal. The tires squealed on the asphalt, and a plume of white smoke drifted up from the back when he glanced at the side mirror.

"Romeo—"

"I'm trying."

"Okay, stop. You're gonna blow a hole in the tires."

Reluctantly, he eased off the gas pedal and snarled and his eyes flashing their dangerous silver light that always happened before a shift. "I thought the network tracker on you was gone."

"Yeah, so did I. But I don't think this guy's with the Black Heron."

"What makes you think that?" He looked at her with wide eyes. "The dude jumped out in front of us to keep us from going anywhere. Wait for it. The attacks will come any minute now."

"No." With her hand hidden from the creature's view, Lily summoned her favorite attack spell. The red sparks flaring to life at her fingertips but she wouldn't use it yet. "Does that look like a beckoning wave to you?"

"Lily, by now, I think we're past the whole 'come closer because I'm giving you a friendly wave' trap."

"But he's not doing anything." The minute she said it, the creature lowered its hand and the green light that kept the Winnie from moving blinked out. Calm and unperturbed, it stood there and waved again for them to step out and join it.

Romeo clenched the steering wheel even tighter and scowled at the creature in the road who very much looked like a giant frog walking upright on two legs. "Fine." He released the steering wheel with a grunt and frowned at

Lily. "You know I won't play nice if this is some kinda trick."

She unbuckled her seatbelt and slowly released it, staring at their unexpected visitor. "I know. But I don't think it's a trick."

With a sigh, he unbuckled his seatbelt and stood from the driver's seat. "Let's go see what it wants, then."

Lily followed him to the top of the steps at the side door and stopped him with a firm hand on his wrist. "Maybe let me go out first, huh? I don't want you to rip that little guy apart simply for sneezing."

His frown deepened, but he shrugged and let her step outside ahead of him.

TWO

As she stepped around the front of the Winnie, Lily made no attempt to hide the red sparks that crackled along her fingertips, but she didn't exactly brandish them, either. The green-skinned being still stood about ten feet from the RV and seemed not to notice her ready attack spell until she'd stopped in front of the Winnie's bumper. Romeo stopped beside her and glared at the oddity in their path.

"You definitely have our attention," she said and raised an eyebrow. "Would you care to explain why?"

"Now, now." The frog-like man raised partially webbed hands in surrender. "You can put that little sparky trick back inside, yes?"

The young couple shared a glance, and the werewolf shook his head barely enough for her to see it. She turned toward the green guy in front of them—she settled on it being a he simply by his voice—and wrinkled her nose. "I definitely don't want to use it." She raised her hand a little to make her point. "But I will if I have to."

"Why did you stop up us in the middle of the road?" Her companion's growl was low and threatening enough to make her brush the back of her hand briefly against his arm in warning.

Give the thing a chance, Romeo.

"Yes, yes, I kept you here. Right here." The frogman pointed at the asphalt below his feet and shuffled side to side. "I am the Watcher. We can be friends."

Lily tilted her head and regarded him suspiciously. "The watcher of what?"

"All things that feel important." The frogman uttered a throaty, gurgling cackle that cut off abruptly. "I am watching you."

Romeo clenched his hands into fists. "See? I knew this wasn't simply a friendly visit."

"Well, we're still trying to determine that," she muttered. "Unless he throws another spell our way, try to hold back." He snorted but kept his aggression in check a little longer. "I'm not sure that explanation's gonna cut it, Watcher. We've come a long way to be here, and we still have a little way to go. What do you want?"

"To be friends, yes? I felt your...wanting. Little witch needs a friend. Many friends. Royal needs a witch." Watcher flashed them a wide, gummy pink grin and exposed rows of tiny, sharp teeth. He chuckled and took two quick, bouncing steps forward.

"That's close enough." The werewolf growled.

"Yes, yes." The creature raised his hands again and

nodded his wide, flat head. "A witch needs a way across the sea. That is your wanting. I saw it. I know it."

Lily leaned toward her companion and whispered, "Do you get any funky magic off this guy? He looks like he might explode too."

He shook his head. "I only smell fish."

The young witch wrinkled her nose and nodded. "You've been spying on us and heard that we need to get across the Mediterranean. That's not the best way to start off a new friendship."

"Not spying. Watching and feeling. The Vátra can help with the sea. An Optatus witch can help with the Royal's wanting too."

Lily grimaced. *Great. The little green frog-guy knows exactly what kind of magic I have running through my veins.*

"If he knows that much, Lil, what else has he seen?" Romeo narrowed his eyes and leaned forward to peer at the creature half his height in the middle of the road. "How long have you been watching us?"

The being's huge eyes shifted left from left to right and he nodded briskly. "Two days. After leaving the fighters, yes? Alone, in that." Watcher pointed at the Winnie behind them. "On the road. I have heard where you wish to be. I have heard why and how and who. Royal has heard of you too, little witch. He wants to help if you want to help." With a nervous smile, the green humanoid wrung his webbed hands and nodded again as he glanced from one to the other. The short silence seemed to indicate that the young couple had no idea what to do with him.

"Spying on us for two days." Romeo turned toward Lily and lowered his voice even more. "That's a fair amount to overhear. And I have a hard enough time understanding what he's saying anyway."

Lily leaned toward him and whispered, "I think he wants to make a deal."

"Yes! A deal. With Royal." Watcher squeaked and jumped from foot to foot.

The werewolf's nostrils flared and he deliberately forced himself not to look at the creature. "Do you think that's a good idea? The guy's pants are made of seaweed."

She tried so hard not to laugh at that, but a tiny smirk still broke through. "He's not attacking us or trying to steal anything, so it might be worth it." When she shrugged, his scowl only darkened. "It's worth finding out a little more, right?" He wouldn't have had an answer for that, even if she'd given him the time to respond before she turned to Watcher and released the attack spell that danced along her fingers. She folded her arms. "Are you saying this Royal can get us and our RV across the Mediterranean in exchange for our help?"

"Your help. Yes. Only yours, little witch—"

"That's not gonna happen." Romeo's eyes flashed silver, and he took a threatening step toward the green man.

"It won't. It won't! You can come too, doggie."

"What did you call me?"

"Okay, time out." Lily took three steps forward in case she had to put herself between Romeo and Watcher should this misunderstanding get too out of control.

"First, let's get rid of the pet names. I'm Lily. This is Romeo."

The creature nodded vigorously with wide eyes.

"And you are?"

"The Watcher. Only Watcher. Always Watcher." He finished with his unnerving grin again, and Lily forced herself not to grimace in response.

"Watcher. Got it." She glanced at Romeo with raised eyebrows and waited for him to look at her. Finally, the silver blinked out of his green eyes flecked with gold, and he rolled his eyes. *That's about as much consent as I'm gonna get right now, I think.* "So, Watcher, what help from me does the...Royal want?"

"Helping. Yes. Only come to talk. To see Royal and listen and understand. Vátra can help you in the water after this." Watcher waved to them again and his webbed hand spun over and over as he jerked his head toward the side of the highway and the cliffs leading into the sea.

"Lily, I don't know if anyone who says, 'We only wanna talk' actually means it like that."

"But if this Royal, whoever it is, can actually help us get across all that"—she gestured toward the glittering sea on their left—"for only a little chat in return, how bad can it be? And we're not exactly on the kind of road trip where we can take our time and hunt through different barges until we find the perfect fit. It could save us considerable time."

"So much time," Watcher squeaked. "We are close. I am fast. Lily and Romeo can be fast. Take time to come with me. Speak to Royal. Listen. And then you'll be all the way." He pointed across the Mediterranean just like Lily had.

He sent the creature another scowl. "Something tells me he doesn't know half of what he's saying."

"I don't know... He might deserve a little more credit." Lily studied Watcher again and tried to smile, but it was thin-lipped and a little skeptical. "I think we should do it."

The werewolf's head whipped toward her, his eyes wide with disbelief. "Are you serious?"

"If we're really that close, it beats an hour and a half drive for the fairly high chance that we'll be turned away from shipyard after shipyard, right?" She pressed her fist slowly into his chest in a teasing nudge. "Besides, I am always ready to make deals with magicals first. And I've never met one of these before. I don't think I've ever even heard of them."

"Vátra!" Watcher pounded his bare chest with a webbed fist and elicited a wet squelch. "Warriors. Negotiators. Swimmers." He winked.

Lily snorted. "I think we can call this a fairly safe detour. And it might save us considerable time, which is really what we need right now." She caught Romeo's green-eyed gaze and held it. "I don't mind meeting with a group of green dudes I've never heard of if it means getting to the other side of that water and finding my mom that much sooner."

With a deep breath, he closed his eyes. When he opened them again, he sighed and held her shoulders gently. "I know. And you're right, but that doesn't mean I have to trust the spy frog."

"That's totally fair." She smirked and shot him a sideways glance as she turned her attention toward their new acquaintance again. "But don't pounce on him, okay?"

He scoffed. "I don't pounce."

"Yes, please, do not." Watcher had returned to wringing his hands but still swayed from side to side and stared at them with expectant hope. "You will come?"

"Yeah." Lily nodded, held the Vátra's gaze, and searched for any sign of deception there. She didn't find any, but in a magical she'd never seen and didn't know existed, she couldn't exactly be sure what deception looked like. "We'll come with you but only to talk."

"Yes, yes. Only. Follow me and do not jump too far." Wiggling his head in delight, Watcher waved them forward with an urgent hand and hurried across the sparse, brittle-looking grasses that grew along the cliffs.

In some way, she had expected their new companion to hop like an actual frog toward the edge of the precipice. Watcher didn't so much walk as march over the rough terrain, his wide, flat head thrown back, his dark-green chest puffed out in front of him, and his scrawny green arms swinging at his sides. She shared another glance with Romeo and had to look away again before she succumbed to laughter. "I'm actually really glad I don't know everything about every magical race in this world."

He stared at her. "Why?"

"It keeps things interesting." With a smirk, she gestured toward the short green man who had already covered a fair distance and bowed. "After you."

The werewolf took a deep breath, shook his head, and walked slowly after their unexpected guide.

She turned toward the Winnie and nodded. "Don't worry. I didn't forget about you." She clapped her hands together and pulled them apart to cast an illusion spell that stretched as a purple, glistening film between her palms. When she'd pulled her hands all the way apart, she flicked her fingers toward the vehicle, and a glistening purple dome wrapped the entire RV. It flashed once and in the next moment, both the purple light and the Winnebago were gone. "Out of sight but definitely not out of mind." She pointed at their home on wheels. "We'll be back."

THREE

The couple stopped beside Watcher at the edge of the cliffs about half a mile south of where they'd left the Winnie. The creature closed his eyes and sniffed loudly at the sea air that swept briskly over the cliffs.

Romeo frowned. "He couldn't have stopped us before we drove past this apparently special location?"

"I'm sure he had his reasons."

"I have many." Their guide turned toward them and spread his scrawny arms. "One reason makes me wait to see what you will do, yes?" The ridges above the creature's bulging eyes wiggled.

If the little guy had eyebrows... Lily turned toward her friend and pursed her lips. "See? He wanted to make sure of us too."

"Now I am sure." Watcher nodded and gazed out over the sea again. "Now we go down."

"Down where?" Romeo peered over the edge of the cliff to where a few white rocks jutted from the water closer to the land. A little farther to the right, the water was darker and obviously far deeper. "What are we supposed to be looking at—"

Their odd companion clapped his webbed hands above his head with a splat and leapt from the edge of the cliff into a straight, neat dive. The werewolf stepped quickly away from the precipice and rolled his eyes. She chuckled and watched the creature's descent until the huge, bare, webbed feet disappeared into the blue-black waters with almost no splash whatsoever.

"Yeah, there's no way I'll follow like that." Romeo shook his head vehemently.

"Relax." The young witch studied the edge of the cliff to the left and the right. "It looks like we have two options."

"Jump like a couple of lunatics or go back to the Winnie, right?"

She shot him a sideways glance and spread her arms wide. "I'm fairly sure I could whip up a decent levitation spell for heavy lifting."

"Hey. It's all muscle."

"Or we can pick out way down that little protruding part over there." Lily pointed at the few feet of the cliffside that stuck out farther over the ocean than the rest of the relatively straight cliff face. "I bet that little corner has good handholds, and we won't have to attempt to go straight down. Mostly."

He squinted at the area she'd indicated. "Yeah, it looks a little less drop-straight-to-our-watery-deaths."

"Wow, you're really mister negative today." She folded

her arms and tilted her head to fix him with a challenging look. "Did you sleep okay?"

"I slept perfectly." He smirked when he recalled what they'd done together the night before that had resulted in the perfect sleep afterward. "I merely don't like where this is headed. I'd say something smells fishy, Lil, but we're literally standing above the sea, and our new little...friend probably eats only fish. I feel like I'm the one who needs to wear the cautious pants right now."

Lily glanced at his jeans and pressed her lips together. "Most pants do look good on you."

"Friends!" The shout from below was swept away a little by the wind and the dull crash of waves against the cliffs. "You are coming?"

"Plus, the way he talks gets under my skin." He shuddered.

"Yeah, the translation spell didn't quite catch this one all the way, I think. But it's close enough."

"I bet his language sounds like walking through mud."

She put a hand on her hip and tilted her head. "I'm not gonna tell you that you can't have your opinion. You're entitled to it, but maybe save the judgments until when we learn what this little guy and his people actually want. Right?"

For a few seconds, he simply stared at her. "I feel like you're taking this somewhere very specific."

"Well..." She shrugged. "You know what it's like to have people walk in the opposite direction when they see a werewolf headed their way simply because they think they know what you want."

Romeo uttered a frustrated grunt. "Yeah, okay. Way to hit that pressure point, Lil."

"I'm only trying to give this guy the benefit of the doubt because we all deserve it."

"I can't even play devil's advocate on this one." He raised an eyebrow at her, then chuckled and turned toward the section of the cliff they'd chosen to scale. She grinned and followed him without another word.

"I see you, friends," Watcher shouted and his flat head bobbed up and down in the deep water. "No jumping from that side or you will not be jumping back up."

"What?" The werewolf glanced at the water below them and the little green face in a sea of blue. "Can you actually jump all the way—never mind. We're climbing." He pointed at the rocky edge below them. "It's gonna take a minute."

"When was the last time you went rock climbing?" Lily asked while she waited on the solid ground and watched him turn cautiously on his hands and knees.

Romeo dug his fingers into the dry earth and kicked a boot out behind him to find a foothold. "I don't know. A year, at least."

"Are you sure you wouldn't rather go the levitation route?"

"And miss the chance to show my skills off?" He tested his weight on the rocks and when he was satisfied they would hold, he brought his other leg down toward the perpendicular cliff face and searched for the next foothold. Before he went any farther, he looked at her and squinted against the sun behind her head. "But you can totally catch me, right? Just in case."

"My reaction time's excellent." She tried to give him a stern nod, but a laugh escaped her anyway.

"Right. I do actually trust you with my life, you know." He didn't look at her and focused instead on the jagged sections of rock that formed the perfect crevices to dig his fingers into and lower himself toward the sea. Still, they both knew he meant it.

"Yeah, I know." Lily lowered herself into a squat at the top of the cliff and watched him intently. "Me too."

By the time he had climbed down enough to move sideways along the cliff, leaving her sufficient space to start her own descent without the possibility of sending any loose pebbles or a shoe down on his head, Watcher had grown ridiculously impatient. The green-skinned Vátra dove beneath the water's surface over and over and emerged a few seconds later to inspect their progress and shout, "Closer!"

After about five minutes of this, Romeo paused. His fingers felt raw as they dug into the rock, and he glanced at the frogman who still bobbed in the water. "I'll get there when I get there, man. But if you yell—"

"Closer!" Watcher croaked and slapped a wet hand over his wide mouth and sank into the water until only his huge eyes showed.

"Okay, one more time after that, I'll...show you what close really is."

Lily snorted a few feet above him and to the right. "Good one."

"I have a hard time multitasking."

The young witch found herself in quite the opposite situation. She'd found an easy and efficient rhythm to find a foothold, swing her other leg down, and cement her grip in the jagged cliff a little with a physical binding spell beneath her fingertips. She hadn't had to use her own magic to help with the climb until she'd descended halfway. The rockface looked much sturdier than it was, for the most part. Twice now, a handful of thin, eroded rock layers had pulled off in her hand.

It happened again when she tried her weight on the next handhold and showered a rain of light-colored dirt and tiny, flat slabs of rock to tumble into the sea below her. She sucked in a sharp breath and caught herself again on a much sturdier ledge. The cliff flashed pale yellow beneath her hand, and her trust in her own binding spells helped quell the nervous flutter in her belly.

"Oh, I see." Romeo looked up at her. They were only a few feet away from each other now and almost close enough to jump into the deeper pool where Watcher waited for them. "I'm fairly sure magical assistance counts as cheating."

Lily puffed out a breath and couldn't help a little smile, even through her concentration. "It's not cheating if it's part of my skillset. And have you ever really looked at the world's top ten rock-climbers?"

"You mean in person? I never had the chance."

"I bet you at least one of them is a magical of some kind."

Shaking his head, he edged sideways along the cliff, and a minute later, she had reached the same level along the wall of rock. Watcher still dove under the waves every minute or two to disappear for a few seconds before he popped his head up and staring with agonized impatience at their progress. But at least he'd taken Romeo's warning seriously.

"All right. I'm gonna call it." The werewolf glanced over his shoulder to see the little green creature almost directly beneath him and about ten feet down. "This is like the high dive."

"Right here. Come right here." Watcher stabbed his finger into the dark water in front of him. He splashed himself in the face without seeming to notice it at all.

"Yeah, I assumed that when you jumped from all the way up there." He turned toward Lily a few feet away and raised his eyebrows. "The holds are quite wet from here down. It's probably safer to simply let go."

She chuckled and stretched for the next handhold beside her. "You go first. I'm gonna wait until I'm over deep water and not jagged rocks."

"You know that's what I meant." With a final glance at the green head bobbing in the water, Romeo shouted, "Okay, Watcher. Watch this!"

The eager Vátra pushed his whole head out from under the surface, grinned, and opened his mouth to shout something in reply. His eyes grew incredibly wide when Romeo lurched off the side of the cliff and fell toward the waves. The werewolf's arms and legs flailed in the air with no control whatsoever. Watcher didn't quite manage to get out of the way fast enough, and the man met the water in something close to a complete back flop. Lily winced at the smack and the gargle of surprise from the little green guy, and she watched the bubbling surface for a few seconds before both Romeo and their guide broke the surface again.

"You're next, Lil," her friend shouted. "It's really not that bad."

"I do not agree." For the first time, Watcher frowned and shot a decidedly unamused glance at the werewolf who'd landed on top of him. The expression looked incredibly strange on a creature without eyebrows.

"Hey, you're fine." Romeo gave him a quick glance and a dismissive wave through the water with a little splash. "I mostly missed you."

Shaking her head, Lily sidled a few more feet until she was more or less where Romeo had leapt from the cliff. "Ready?"

"Yes, yes!" their guide shouted. "Always ready."

Her friend shot him a skeptical glance, and she launched herself from the rock. She spun enough in the air to face the others and brought her legs together and her arms close to her sides seconds before she reached the water. It took her longer than she would've liked to kick her way to the surface. With a deep breath and the seawater spraying into her open mouth, she swiped the water out of her eyes and grinned. "That was fun."

"Your fun is too slow." Watcher glanced at each of his new companions and pointed farther down the cliffs where the waves were even calmer. "This way," he said briskly before he dove out of sight and disappeared.

"Too slow?" Romeo met her gaze with wide eyes. "The dude didn't even get outta the way when I jumped."

She shoved a wall of seawater at his face and laughed, kicking her legs to tread water in the deep pool surrounded by so many sharp rocks protruding from the surface. "It's much warmer than I thought."

"It feels like home, huh?"

"A little. Come on." She nodded toward where Watcher had pointed before the green-skinned Vátra popped up and waved frantically at them again. "I don't know how long our little friend's patience is gonna hold out."

They swam toward the green head and bulging eyes that watched their progress and moved as quickly as they could in the waves that surged against the high rise of cliffs. When they finally reached Watcher, he smacked his lips and pointed at the rock. "Down. Through. Up. Yes?"

"Um..." Romeo blew a splash of water off his mouth and frowned. "Can we try that again?"

"Follow me, friends. Inside." With that, the Vátra ducked beneath the dark water again and disappeared.

"So there's gotta be a cave down there or something, right?"

Lily nodded. "That's what I think." She summoned a bright-white orb of light in her palm, took a deep breath, and submerged in pursuit of their guide. Her magical light illuminated another two feet of solid rock wall below her before it disappeared into a dark, gaping hole underwater.

She flicked the light orb from her hand and sent it ahead of her into what was definitely an underwater tunnel.

The passage was narrow enough to make her feel slightly claustrophobic, but it was thankfully short. But the time the ceiling angled upward again toward the surface, her lungs were already burning. She came up with a gasp and a few more sputtered breaths and blinked away the saltwater until she saw Watcher slopping his webbed-footed way up another beach of white sand ahead.

Something brushed against her ankle, and she pushed herself forward so Romeo had enough room to come up behind her. He shook his head and sprayed water everywhere, and together, they looked at the fairly large cavern rising above them.

"Yep. Totally a cave." He shot her a glance and headed toward the white sand that rimmed the water.

Smirking, Lily followed him. Her floating orb of light bobbed on the surface and she waved it toward the beach before her shoes found purchase on the slope toward the beach. Watcher jumped at the sight of his own shadow dancing against the far wall in front of him, and he whirled with high-pitched croak. "Is that yours?" he hissed.

The couple waded as quickly as they could onto the sandbar that stretched across the center of the cavern. "It was only to help us see the way in," she said. "We don't see as well in the dark as you do."

Romeo gave her a playful frown and muttered, "Speak for yourself."

"Put it away." Watcher swatted at her magical light

and had to turn away, grimacing. "Too much light means too much light. We do not need another sun."

"Sorry." She pressed her lips together and flicked a finger at the bright white ball of light. It fizzled and cast them in complete darkness as they stood at the highest point of the sandbar. *And now I can't see anything. Wait a minute...*

As her vision adjusted, Lily stared at the previously darkened water on the other side of this small strip of land. It glowed with a soft, green luminescence that flashed over the ripples as Watcher waded back down the other side of the sandbar and toward the green light. "Don't fight," he said and looked at them one more time with a nod. "Only follow." He slipped out of sight again, his body a dark silhouette against the green glow, and swam quickly down and away from them again.

"And how many perfectly harmless creatures warn their friends not to fight?" Romeo wiggled a finger in his ear and shook his head and his entire body before he stepped into the water once again.

She smirked. "I don't know. Maybe the kind who's completely aware of your skepticism and has no problem imagining your knee-jerk reaction." She moved forward cautiously and realized that the water was slightly cooler than what they'd swum through to get there. "So try not fighting first. I'll do the same. Deal?"

Romeo cleared his throat and stared at the last flicker of Watcher's webbed foot as it disappeared through the new, green-lit tunnel. "Deal. Just in case, though, Lil, do you know any underwater breathing spells?"

"Of course I do. Come on." When they walked far enough to bring the level up to their chests, she took a deep breath and dove toward the green light. *I merely haven't had to cast that spell in a long time. And I really hope I won't have to.*

FOUR

Neither one of them could have anticipated the source of the green glow from the tunnel or the water or the massive cavern that opened in front of them on the other side. Strands of luminescent algae clung to the walls of the cave and the rocks below them and pulsed now and then in both darker and lighter shades. A few glowing fish darted in front of them, and Lily looked down at a coral reef beyond the tunnel. Every plant and rock and even the colored pebbles released various intensities of the same green light.

Lily grimaced as the saltwater stung her eyes more than she had expected it would. Below her, the edge of the reef dropped off into a massive level area. Glowing blue domes rose from the bottom of the cavern hundreds of feet down, and she caught a glimpse of a few green-skinned bodies that darted here and there between the domes and what looked like buildings underwater.

A spray of bubbles and a grunt of surprise traveled

thickly through the water. She turned to see Romeo trying to swim backward away from a giant green bubble that hurtled toward him through the water. She wanted to call to him, but that would have left her with a lungful of seawater. *Where's Watcher?*

She located him immediately inside the opening of the tunnel where he hovered beside the rock wall and watched the green bubble pursue her friend. The little creature's eyes were wide with concern, but he did nothing to help.

Lily's lungs felt like they were about to burst now, and she sent a streak of her red crackling sparks toward the determined orb. She didn't have the time to see what happened and immediately kicked toward the surface as she needed to get above water so she could breathe. When she reached toward the darkness overhead, her hands thumped against the slightly bumpy, slick ceiling of the cavern, which was entirely filled with water. *There's no air.*

She dropped down again and saw Watcher, still beside the wall and now focused on her. *Romeo was right. This was totally a trap.* She tried to ignore her aching lungs and the desperate need to breathe as she struggled toward the reef and the opening of the tunnel. It was short enough that she could get through and out to the sea again, where she knew there was air.

Watcher fixed his wide-eyed gaze on her and thumped his webbed palm against a round notch in the stone wall. A blast of green bubbles spewed from a crevice beside him. In under a second, they'd all combined to form a massive orb as big as the one that pursued Romeo. This one headed in her direction.

Lily swam as fast as she could, but her heart pounded in her chest and echoed in her head, which made her dizzy. The pursuing orb was only inches behind her, but that was much closer than the tunnel opening still a foot ahead. *Why would he bring us down here simply to kill us?*

The bubble touched the toes of her flats and sent a cool, tingling wave all the way up her limbs. She felt it rise higher and higher through her body before she fell through actual air and right onto a soft, bouncing substance that gave a little under her weight. Everything was simply a green glow, and although her head hadn't quite caught up with what had happened, her body took over the way it was supposed to.

The young witch retched where she hunched over on hands and knees. Seawater and coffee splashed over her hands and disappeared through the strange luminescence. Lily gasped and took huge, desperate gulps of air before her body accepted that it was, in fact, getting oxygen. She spewed the last of the seawater from her mouth, and as the bright glow around her faded away into a much clearer, duller translucence, she caught sight of Watcher hovering in front of her and staring fixedly at her with his huge eyes.

"What the hell was that?" she shouted.

"I said do not fight, Lily witch." The Vátra's voice wavered a little underwater as if it echoed from somewhere very far away. "I should have said to listen and remember too." He spread his arms expressively.

"What?" She noticed a slimy-looking trail of something floating away from her and realized it was her vomit moving through the water. With a grimace, she sat and looked at the top of the translucent dome around her. The faint, glowing green color was still barely visible. "The bubbles were to help us. Right. Yeah, Watcher, that would've been really good to explain before we thought we were done for."

"Done with what?"

She shook at the green-skinned creature. "Never mind. Where's Romeo?"

The layer around her, which had grown much smaller in the last few seconds and narrowing closer around her body, jiggled from an impact behind her. She turned quickly. Romeo floated in the underwater cavern and gave off a faint green hue. "Sorry." He slapped the protective barrier as it shrank into shape around his arms, then patted his head. "This thing's a little hard to drive until it's diving-suit-shaped."

Lily looked up again as the top of her bubble settled over her face. That cold tingle flashed across her entire body again before she peered through a green-tinged film at all the underwater life around them. "Are you okay?"

He glanced at her and nodded a few times before he widened his eyes. "It's only a little hard to adjust to full-body contacts. But yeah, I'm good. You?"

"I wish I'd brushed up on that underwater-breathing spell before we got here." She shrugged, which felt strangely weird in a magical airsuit.

"Next time," Romeo said, pointing at the Vátra treading water with a sheepish smile, "you should tell people not to fight the bubbles because they'll *help us live.*

Leaving that information out is a lot more trouble than it's worth."

"No trouble. No. No trouble at all for friends." Watcher nodded vigorously and extended his long, webbed fingers to pluck at the magical membrane fitted to her shoulder. "These are your gills."

"That's a weird thought." She glanced at the green membrane on her arm. *And what's it gonna leave behind when we get outta here?*

"Time to go, friends. Royal is waiting for you and your talk and your help." He waved them forward and darted toward the edge of the reef and down into the expansive cavern.

"Maybe slow down a little," Romeo called after the creature. He caught up to Lily and swam behind her in the wake of Watcher's swift, powerful kicks with his webbed feet. "Does that look like some kinda city to you?"

"You know, I actually thought that before I thought I might drown." She glanced at him and raised her eyebrows. "But yes. It looks like a city."

"This isn't, like...Atlantis or anything, is it?"

Lily chuckled and pulled herself through the water after their Vátran guide. "I'm fairly sure Atlantis is way out in the middle of the Atlantic Ocean—hence the name—and not in an underwater cave beneath cliffs in Greece."

"Wait. But it actually exists?"

"As far as I know, yeah. Ancient civilizations aren't as secret as most people think." She looked at him over her shoulder as he swam with halting breaststrokes and paused every few seconds to try to piece together the new information.

"What about aliens?"

She burst out laughing. The magical film around her vibrated against her lips and she grimaced. "Are you asking me if aliens built the pyramids?"

"What I mean is that if Atlantis is real, what else is?"

"I'm reasonably sure we didn't have any help from extraterrestrials. But it wouldn't surprise me if most of the people involved somehow in the Wonders of the World were magicals. Please tell me it wouldn't surprise you, either."

"No. That makes sense." He caught up to her, and they dove farther down toward the bottom of the cavern. Schools of glowing fish hurried past them, and the water seemed to grow even warmer the closer they moved to the blue domes. "You know, Lil, we've seen so much crazy stuff on this trip. It never even crossed my mind that we'd swim to an underwater city in magical bodysuits to talk to a giant green frogman about making a deal to get us somewhere else."

"I can't blame you for not having thought of everything." Lily brushed her hand against his shoulder, but the bubbles surrounding them bounced off each other and she only felt the vibration of her own magical breathing apparatus shiver over her body. "Okay, touching anything is really weird right now."

Romeo smirked. "I wouldn't call that a plus."

"Friends!" Watcher darted toward them out of

nowhere and hovered less than a foot away from Lily. She pushed herself back in the water and stared at him.

"Okay, little guy," Romeo told their guide, "I know her literal bubble is about half an inch around her, but the personal bubble rule still applies."

The creature merely fixed them each with a firm stare. "Stay close to me. Getting lost is not as hard as it seems."

The werewolf looked around their frog-like guide and peered at all the blue domes of different sizes that dotted the floor of the cavern. Now that they'd come down this far, they could see the domes rising higher and higher into the darkness to the left, although they were less concentrated than the main part of the underwater city ahead of them. "It actually looks like that would be easy."

"So follow, yes?" Watcher pointed first at Romeo, then at Lily before he spun abruptly and darted away toward the largest blue dome in the center of a ring of smaller blue orbs.

"I feel like we're on a kindergarten field trip."

She snorted at her companion's obvious chagrin and set off after the Vátran who was so eager to get them to Royal.

FIVE

When they reached the spaces between the towering structures, it became apparent that tunnels of the same blue glow connected every oversized bubble that comprised the Vátran city. Watcher took them toward one of these tunnels and floated gently down beside the nearest one before he stuck his webbed hand through the luminescent wall. "We go inside." He sent his visitors a pointed glance and slipped through the light and into the tunnel.

"Okay, then." Lily attempted to push her hand through in the same way, but her membrane-coated fingers simply bounced off.

Romeo snorted. "Something tells me these little green guys haven't had to make many adjustments down here for people who actually need to breathe." He kicked closer to her and the tunnel's outer wall. "Or we simply need a harder push, right?" Before she could respond, he drew his arm back, focused on the barrier, and launched his fist at it.

The resultant thud echoed in an oddly distorted way and the force if the contact hurtled him through the water. He tumbled head over heels until he bounced against the wall of a smaller dome and drifted back to her.

"That was definitely a cool trick."

He shook his head. "Totally unintentional, but I'll take cool."

Lily laughed and turned to face the tunnel to try again. A streak of green burst out into the water beside her and two huge, cold things pressed up against her back. Watcher's powerful kick launched her into the wall and she squeezed through it with a slurping sound and a spray of water that landed beside her on the tunnel floor. She had no time to even attempt to break her fall, although the magical film that covered her entire body kept her from really hurting herself. "Shock-absorbing air-suit bubbles. Okay..." As she pushed herself off her knees, the blue glow trembled and spit Romeo out with the same wet slurp.

The werewolf landed with a grunt but was back on his feet in seconds. He glared at the dark, wavering silhouette that quickly moved closer and larger against the hazy blue barrier. His hands curled turned into as much of a fist as he could make them but the film around his body was thick enough to keep his fingers from fully closing.

"Okay, maybe take a breath." Lily stepped toward him.

The dark silhouette outside pressed against the tunnel and slipped easily and smoothly through. Watcher dropped to his webbed feet with a wet slap, although no cascade of extra water sneaked in with his entrance. The

Vátra turned to face his guests and spread his arms. "You have never used one of these?"

The werewolf scowled. "I've never been kicked through a wall by a talking frog, either. Don't do that again."

"Ha!" The creature looked from Romeo to Lily and back again, then pointed a webbed finger with a sharp, yellowed nail at her. "If she kicked you through, you would laugh and wonder and say, 'More luck when I do this again.'"

"I trust her," he told their guide. "I don't trust you."

Watcher narrowed his huge eyes, then shrugged. "You do not matter so much." The Vátra waved them on to follow him down the luminescent hallway.

Lily snorted. "My translation spell is definitely not up to speed with Vátran."

Romeo gritted his teeth and snarled silently at the green-skinned creature. Quickly, he glanced at her and tried not to smile at her. "He was totally right, though. I wouldn't mind if you kicked me through a wall."

"Oh, really?" She nodded after their guide, who now marched down the seawater-slickened hall. "That probably depends on why I'm kicking you and where."

"Okay, let's not get too super-creative with that fantasy, huh?" He squared his shoulders and nodded. "I'm just sayin'."

"Come on." Lily increased her pace, impressed by the shifting colors of the floors. One second, they looked like flattened coral, and the next, they might have been glass in an aquarium. Every now and then, the pattern looked something more like seaweed, and the coloring faded smoothly from orange to glistening silver to yellow and then brown, over and over in a seemingly endless cycle. Her companion walked beside her down the empty hallway but after a moment, they began to squeak.

"You gotta be kidding me." The werewolf picked his foot up and examined the bottom of his boot still covered by the film of the breathing suit. "It looks like we dried up."

"I won't even consider getting us out of these bubble things until we're back on land." She twisted her shoe on the floor of the hallway and elicited a loud, obnoxious squeak with every movement. "If we can be pushed into this tunnel, we can be pushed out. I'm not even sure if the underwater spells I know will actually work if they're also cast underwater."

Romeo sighed. "Good point. It looks like we'll make a noisily noble entrance, then."

She fought down a laugh, but a bubbling chuckle escaped her anyway.

Up ahead, Watcher's face poked out from behind the corner of the blue-lit hallway. His eyes bulged wider than normal, and he glanced constantly behind him as he waved them frantically forward. "You will be old before you get here. I will be old. Royal will be—" He stopped abruptly as if he couldn't believe he was about to abuse Royal's name in casual comments. "Come, come, come!"

With a shared nod, Lily and Romeo moved swiftly down the hallway toward their guide. Their footsteps squealed but their individual rhythms weren't even close to being in line with each other. They both fought back explosions of laughter, which was even harder to do when Watcher glared at their suits. The creature shook his head rapidly and his mouth opened as if to speak before he simply smacked his own forehead with a wet slap and disappeared around the corner in front of them.

"Do you think they're gonna take you any less seriously because we sound like this?" Romeo muttered.

"I hope so. If the Royal wants my help so badly, he should probably add improvements to his welcome package."

The only thing he could do besides dissolve into laughter again was to clear his throat and press his lips tightly together.

When they rounded the corner, Watcher now stood in an archway at the end of the tunnel, his heels thumped together, his back straight, and one arm stretched toward them in an invitation. The shifting floor beneath him now flashed with pulsing lights, one color after the other, that moved toward the room beyond the tunnel as if inviting the guests to enter. Orange, yellow, brown, and green flashed across their guide's face as he stared at their approach.

They passed the green-skinned creature and the breathing film beneath their feet still made obscene noises. Watcher hissed at their shoes, then snapped to attention again.

The young couple stepped into what had to be the largest central dome of the Vátran city. It rose hundreds of feet above them and cast a much mellower blue glow through the room than what they'd walked through in the tunnels. Stone pools filled with water shimmered throughout the room, some of them filled with aquatic plants and flowers and others completely empty. These occasionally flashed a bright hue of orange or silver but for the most part, they were still. Beyond that, the room was entirely empty.

"I thought you said we would be late," Lily whispered when Watcher passed her and stepped into the massive room.

"We are." Their guide slowed his pace in order to minimize the echoing slap of his webbed feet on the smooth, colorfully shifting floors. "Royal is not in any place first."

Romeo wrinkled his nose. "That must make it tough to find privacy. Does that include bathroom breaks?"

Lily shot him a warning glance. *Don't laugh, Lily.*

"Hey, it's a valid question." He shrugged.

"With a name like Royal, I assume we're here to speak to their leader." The young witch nodded at the oversized cushion at the other side of the apparent throne room, which was shaped like a lily pad and appeared to be a few feet bigger than her bed. "That and the fact that our friend's name's Watcher, and he told us he literally watches."

The werewolf tilted his head in acknowledgment. "It makes sense. That throne cushion over there looks pretty, right? Royal's gotta be a big dude, then."

"What makes you think that?"

"Well, these guys are..." He glanced around the throne room, which remained empty except for Watcher who stood a few yards away between them and the oversized cushion. "Frog people," he whispered. "Frog leaders are big, right? Like bullfrogs. And that big general dude in Star Wars who slobbered everywhere when he—actually, he shook exactly like a dog."

"That's what you're basing your assumption on?" Lily folded her arms, which stuck together and squeaked at the film-on-film contact so she dropped them hastily to her sides. "CG Star Wars characters."

"If you have any insider information, Lil, I'm all ears."

She had to look away from him and pretend to be insanely interested in the closest stone pool, which released one purple bubble every few seconds from the very center. The ensuing ripples flashed in silver and orange, and when the bubble burst, it ejected a tiny puff of purple mist that dissipated quickly into the air. *Actually, that's really interesting.* "I think we should dial down on the jokes," she muttered. "We've met storytellers and Romani and life-giving witches who teleport through the earth, but something tells me the Vátran won't pick up on your sense of humor."

"Ours."

"What?"

"Our sense of humor. We'll split this fifty-fifty." Romeo wiggled his eyebrows.

"Sure. And the same goes for whatever impression we leave on this Royal person, deal?"

He shifted quickly to face her, his film-covered boots making their customary obnoxious squeal, and stuck his hand out. "Deal."

Lily didn't think before she reached out to shake his hand. Their palms bounced off each other with a much louder clap than a normal handshake should ever make. The witch glanced down at her hand and frowned as the film vibrated until it settled again. "This stuff is so weird."

Romeo shook his hand and made a face like he tried to fling slime onto the floor. "You're tellin' me. I feel like a walking pile of Jell-O." He caught her sharp glance and cleared his throat. "Sorry."

Quick footsteps slapped across the floor from across the throne room and to their left. The floors of the tunnel connected on that side flashed with bright pinks and oranges, faster and faster toward the throne room. Half a dozen Vátran people spilled into the massive blue dome. Three of them carried long spears twice their own height that looked like they were made of bone. One of them trotted along with a stone tray of food Lily wouldn't even dare Romeo to eat. The other two ran in with folds of shimmering cloth piled high in their arms. The six creatures fanned out around the giant cushion in the back of the throne room, and the one holding the tray of food bellowed, "He is coming now. The Royal is here. He is presenting to you and is supreme himself." The being's voice was surprisingly high-pitched and warbly, made even more so by the trembling echo it cast around the dome.

The werewolf leaned toward her. "No one will win the vocabulary award here."

"Stop." She pressed her lips together and stared straight ahead.

SIX

Watcher paced continually in front of his guests. His feet barely made a sound on the floor now and he clasped his webbed hands behind his back. All the Vátran who had gathered faced the tunnel beside the throne cushion as the colors flashed brighter and brighter until Lily had to look away.

A tall, incredibly slim figure stepped from the entrance, only a few inches away from scraping his head against the top of the archway. The flashing streaks of orange, pink, and silver winked out immediately to reveal the constant glow of the tunnel beyond once more. Slowly and almost carelessly, the tall Vátran made his way to the others who waited in front of the cushion, his hands clasped behind his back.

This one did have a greenish coloring to it, which was mostly around the edges of his face and the tops of his shoulders. Every other inch of its skin pulsed with different colors—beside the brownish-green, a deep gold traced along the creature's neck, collarbone, and inner arms. The edges of his chest and stomach were a bright yellow that faded almost into a neon-orange and then a blinding hot-pink in the very center of his torso. This Vátran was lithe but not starved-looking and a hint of muscles showed within the bare pecks and abs. A loincloth made of the same seaweed-looking material as Watcher's frayed pants dangled between his slender legs and his feet weren't anywhere near as large as the others' despite the creature being almost twice as tall.

When the colorful humanoid—equally as bald as the others but with much smaller and more proportionately sized eyes—reached the cushion flanked by its followers, he turned toward the center of the throne room and regarded the room calmly. "The Royal is come." He lifted one foot back into the middle of the cushion, dragged the other smoothly toward it, and lowered himself fluidly to sit cross-legged. His hands, also hot-pink in the centers, rested palms-up on his knees as if to signify that he was ready.

Someone's gotta be made of rubber to sit like that. Lily studied the Royal with immense curiosity and fought the sudden urge to run toward him and bombard the creature with questions about his entire race. *That's not why we're here.*

After thirty seconds of absolute silence and zero movement, Watcher turned slowly to meet her gaze, then Romeo's. The green-skinned guide held up a hand in a subtle signal to wait before he turned and mimicked the Royal's former pose—slow steps, his head held high, and his hands clasped behind his back.

All around them, the stone pools flashed their brilliant colors beneath the glow of the blue dome. *This is starting to feel like a rave. I thought I left those behind me after high school.*

"Great Royal." Watcher stopped directly in front of the seated monarch and bowed until his wide, flat head almost touched the glistening floors. "The Watcher has brought friends to speak. Lily witch and Romeo werewolf." The creature spread his arms fully to the sides and focused his gaze on the flashing floor inches from his flat nose. "The friends are speaking to receive diávra through the la-lass."

After a few more seconds of absolutely nothing, Watcher straightened fully, stared at the back wall of the dome above the Royal's head, and thrust his arm out toward the young couple. "I think that's our cue," Lily whispered. They moved slowly toward their guide, once again squeaking rhythmically with each step across the throne room floor that now looked like it was made of pink sand with neon-orange ripples. She didn't want to stare at the floor as they approached, but she couldn't help darting glances at the Royal seated cross-legged on the cushion, which was obviously bad form in the Vátran court.

When they reached Watcher's side, the smaller Vátra slapped his hand against his thigh and stepped aside. Another silence followed. The Royal sat as still as a sculpture except for the bright colors of his chest that pulsed with his heartbeat. The young witch shared an uncertain glance with her werewolf friend before she took a deep breath. "Thank you for seeing us." *That's the best way to start out with a royal of any kind. It should be good enough here.*

The Royal's unblinking eyes focused on the opposite wall of the dome and fluttered rapidly. When they opened again, they'd lost their golden-brown hue and the irises were now the same blazing blue as the glowing domes and tunnel walls. His head moved slowly until his gaze rested on Lily and he inclined his head toward her. It wasn't much movement at all, but on a creature who'd made the entrance he had and who hadn't moved at all since he'd sat, it felt like a complete bow. "Greetings, friends." The Royal's voice wasn't overly male or female, which might have stemmed from the fact that he spoke in multiple tones at once, high and low. Judging by anatomy alone, Lily guessed the creature was male. But they weren't dealing with witches or werewolves or even androgynous warlocks at this point. The Vátra were clearly something different.

She offered a slow nod in return, and Romeo cleared his throat when he did the same. The Royal's vibrant gaze never left hers.

"The Watcher has told us of your journey," he said. "As much of it as he has come to learn, although he left out one very important detail. I wish to correct that."

The young witch glanced at Watcher, who stared past her in a straight line toward the side of the throne room, unblinking and unfazed by his leader's words. *He doesn't seem scared, but I hope that statement wasn't a precursor to punishing the little guy.* She glanced at the Royal and waited for more.

"You are no ordinary witch, Lily. And we desire all our

friends to be honest about their true selves." The Vátran leader tilted his head back enough to look up at her down the bridge of his slightly more human-looking nose, however flat it still was. "You are an Optatus, one of very few. It is for this reason that we have asked our Watcher to deliver you our message."

When she took a deep breath, she was keenly aware of how strange it was to feel the air pull into her lungs from the filmy breathing suit wrapped tightly around her. "Yes." She nodded slowly. "That's what I am. Watcher told us that was why you wanted to talk."

"He has seen your true nature, so we have seen it ourselves. We understand that you and your companion wish to cross what the gigni like you call the Mediterranean Sea. This desire is of a sensitive and personal nature to you specifically, is it not?"

"It is." Lily had to take a minute to form her next words. *There's nothing wrong with trusting a goofy Vátra in seaweed pants who dives off cliffs. This one has more power than all of its kind in this room put together.* She stared at those glowing blue eyes. "It's also time-sensitive. Something very important to me was taken to the other side of the sea, and I need to get it back."

"Of course. And something most precious to us has been taken to this side of the sea and onto the land. We also desire its return. Will you hear our proposal, Optatus?" Beyond the Royal's thin, pale-orange lips moving when it spoke, not a single muscle stirred in the rest of its body.

She glanced at Romeo, who muttered, "It's only a

request to listen and something tells me we'll get perfectly understandable explanations this time."

"Good." She turned to the Royal and tried not to let herself become impatient after mentioning how quickly they needed to make it to Libya. "We'll hear it, yes."

For the first time, the Royal's illuminated eyes flickered briefly toward Romeo. "Do you speak for your companion as well?"

"Only when we agree on something," her companion replied, perfectly happy to answer for himself.

The Royal's gaze roamed the curve of the dome over their heads, then settled on the young witch once more. "This precious thing that was stolen from us rests in a temple miles from our home. We cannot travel above as none of our people are strong enough to endure the sun and the winds in the way that gigni endure them. We wish for an Optatus to retrieve that which has been taken from our loving arms—that which is rightfully our own and of the Vátra. When you bring the Varelos to us, we offer safe and swift diávra through the la-lass."

Lily forced herself not to frown. "I'm sorry. I don't understand what that means."

"Travel across this Mediterranean Sea."

There we go. The young witch pretended to consider the offer, though she already knew she'd take it. *I have no problem enduring the sun and wind. It should be easy to retrieve an extra artifact after a literal treasure hunt across three continents.*

Romeo glanced sharply at her and frowned. "You know, our new friend who likes to kick people said all we had to do was come down here for a talk. Now we have to run an errand?"

She drew her gaze slowly away from the Royal and leaned toward the werewolf before she lowered her voice. "I know. This is the actual deal now. It could really help us."

"It could also turn out to be a huge waste of time and get us into trouble we honestly don't need, Lil." He widened his eyes and nodded anyway.

"Is this a binding agreement?" she asked the Royal.

"We offer an invitation to aid one another, Optatus. We both receive what we desire, or neither of us is satisfied."

That doesn't sound like a trick to me. "How quickly would you be able to get us across the sea?"

The Royal closed his eyes again and a bright pink light pulsed on his closed eyelids. "What the gigni mark as one half of an hour."

When she glanced at her friend again, he seemed nonplussed but definitely more cheerful. "Okay, that's definitely an improvement."

"I accept your invitation," she told the Royal. "I'll bring you this...item in return for safe passage across the Mediterranean Sea to Libya." *I can't be too careful when laying out the terms.*

The Royal's eyes opened again slowly, and his gaze drifted away from her toward the far wall of the dome behind her. His thin arm extended to the side and gestured toward one of the colorful pools in the throne room. The rest of the Vátra's body remained perfectly still.

The water in the closest pool bubbled and flashed brilliantly between pink, orange, and silver, and a shape took form within the water rising from its center. "The Varelos," the Royal said in his multiple voices echoing as one. "Precious to the Vátra. To us." The extra water dripped away from the image of a staff floating above the pool and rippling in place. At the top of it, a rounded tip took the shape of an inverted U. Three sharp tines protruded from each side of the U and all six of them pulsed with golden light. "We have felt it in the temples of Oneiroi above the waters, in the land across which you have been traveling, Optatus. You will find it there, as many others have failed to do. And when you return the Varelos to us, where it belongs, we shall deliver you to your destination."

"Okay." She nodded. "If there's anything else I should know about how to retrieve it, I'd appreciate whatever information you have."

"It is precious to the heart and necessary to calm the unseen storms."

Lily paused. She had no idea what that meant but realized the Royal would have explained further if it was necessary. "Thank you," she said instead of her initial urge to ask for more.

"Is there a time limit on this?" Romeo asked.

The Royal lowered his arm from the pool, and the water-formed Varelos returned to the stone basin with a whispering sigh. Not a drop spilled over the edge. "The only limitation is that which one places on oneself."

When she caught the confusion behind her friend's

frown, she leaned toward him and whispered, "That means no."

"I didn't wanna assume—"

"We must take our silence now." Without another word, the Vátra Royal uncrossed his legs and lay back on the massive cushion. He lowered himself one vertebra at a time as his arms sank into the fabric. The pulsing pink light in his chest and abdomen quickened until he'd stretched out fully on his back and stared up at the ceiling of the dome, unmoving. The lights slowed until only the pulsing glow remained and surrounded his body, and nothing else moved.

For a few seconds, she wondered if they would have to show themselves out of the Vátra city and back to the surface. As if on cue, Watcher turned quickly and looked at her. "Out now, friends." He gestured toward the tunnel through which they'd first entered and moved swiftly across the throne room again, still careful to make as little noise as possible with his huge, webbed feet. Lily nodded at the Royal, knowing he couldn't see the movement but guessing that he probably felt it anyway. She nodded for Romeo to do the same, and the werewolf ducked his head in an awkward half-bow before they both turned to follow their guide.

SEVEN

Their return journey was far less painful and uncomfortable in the magical breathing suits but they were both relieved to breathe fresh air again. The couple surfaced on the other side of the cliffs where the sun glinted off the water, and Watcher came up quickly behind them.

Romeo glanced at the tall, jagged face of pale rock and chewed the inside of his cheek. "Do you think we should get rid of these squeaky suits first? I don't think they'll be too helpful for climbing all the way back up."

"I can try." Lily raised her hand to glance at the thin substance still coating her but had to lower it again to keep her afloat while she tread water. "I don't know if my spells will work through this stuff."

"No spells yet." Watcher studied them and his wide eyes creased at the corners when he smiled. "Gigni need to get back up first, yes?"

"That's what we're trying to find a way to do." Romeo

nodded at their green-skinned guide. "Do you have any suggestions?"

"I will get you up. Lily witch, you remember where these cliffs are. That is a promise. Come back with the Varelos for Royal, and I will come back for you. Helping and helping, yes?"

"I can do that." She glanced at the towering cliffs. "Assuming we can get up there at a reasonable time."

"You can!" With a cackle, Watcher raised a webbed green hand and smacked it on the surface of the sea. A green light flared to life before a column of water burst from beneath both Lily and Romeo and hurled them upward dozens of feet and toward the land above the cliffs. She had barely enough time before the dry grasses rushed toward her to fling both hands out and cast a physical compulsion spell on herself. It was meant to slow her ascent but acted as a giant crash pad instead, which made her landing easier than it could have been but still not quite pleasant. She tucked her head and legs and rolled across the dirt and sparse grasses as Romeo skidded face-first across the ground.

"Oh, come on." He grunted annoyance and pulled his hands beneath him to roll and flop onto his back. The geyser of seawater that had launched them back to land fell into the Mediterranean again, the splash only a little louder than the crash of waves against the cliffs. He thumped a hand against his chest and the Vátran diving suit vibrated at the contact. "I'm not saying I'm okay with being shot out of a vertical cannon, but this stuff makes fairly good armor." He studied his hand and turned it from side to side and the translucent green film shimmered in the sunlight.

"Yeah, if you're okay with not being able to cast effective spells or hold a weapon. I don't know if that stuff would hold through a shift, either." She sat and stared absently at the sky as she rubbed the shoulder that had hit the ground first.

"Good point. We'll call it good armor for someone who doesn't know how to protect themselves, then."

"That was definitely us in the Vátran city."

Romeo sighed. "True."

"Are you okay?"

"Physically? Yeah." The werewolf pushed himself up to sit with his legs stretched out in front of him and raised his eyebrows. "I still don't feel too enthusiastic about this little side quest, though."

"I know. We'll simply have to see how it plays out. If it's more trouble than finding a ship to take us across, then no deal." She shrugged and glanced out across the Mediterranean, nothing but glistening waves and blue sky on the horizon.

"Friends!" Watcher's voice barely rose above the constant crash of waves and the few gulls that screeched overhead. Lily glanced at Romeo, and they both struggled to their feet, fighting for balance against the film that still coated their bodies and vibrated with a little bounce against everything they touched.

When they reached the edge of the cliffs, she peered over and cupped her hands around her mouth to shout, "I'll remember."

"Yes, yes. Good! I hope you have all fortune in what you will do, Lily and Romeo friends."

"Thank you."

The werewolf raised his hand for a hesitant wave, confused by why he felt the need to make the gesture to the Vátra anyway. "It's been real, man."

Watcher threw his head back and cackled until a spray of foamy seawater arced into his mouth and made him gurgle. The green-skinned creature seemed completely unfazed by it. "Always real. Always now. For most of it. Do not start dreaming!" He returned the wave, flashed them his wide, gummy, sharp-toothed grin, and dove beneath the water and disappeared.

Romeo shook his head. "There seriously is a gap in the translation spell. He thought I was being literal."

"Well, you both got the general point across. And the Royal didn't seem to have any difficulty at all with vocabulary."

"Yeah, that was a little weird. Do you have any guesses about that?"

Lily shrugged and took a few steps away from the edge of the cliff. "His eyes changed colors right before he spoke to us. You saw that, right?"

"Superdome-blue. Yep."

"I think he either added to my translation spell to make our conversation perfectly clear, or he channeled a similar spell of his own to speak English."

"Huh." Her companion paused a moment in thought. "The little guys didn't seem to think there was anything weird about it."

"Well, they probably didn't understand a word of it. Or the Royal uses unexpected magic like that more than I thought."

"Option three. They've been brainwashed and couldn't have reacted even if they wanted to."

She clicked her tongue and shot him a playful frown. "Come on. Yeah, it was a little weird that none of them spoke or looked at anything but the wall. But I wouldn't go as far as brainwashing." Studying the film on her hands, she walked slowly across the short, scruffy grasses and salty dirt and each step made her bounce a little. "They're a completely different race so it makes sense that they'd have a completely different culture. And I don't know exactly how their magic works. But Watcher didn't seem scared taking us into that throne room or whatever they call it. I think that's simply the way things are with the Vátra."

"Well, to each his own." Romeo nodded at her hands. "Do you think you can get this stuff off? Our green friend forgot to leave an instruction manual."

She smirked. "I don't think there is one, but..." Her hand twisted one way, then the other, and she grinned. "I get to experiment with something completely new."

"Not on me first, I hope."

With a low chuckle, she met his gaze and tried to put her hands on her hips. Her palms, of course, simply bounced off, and he snorted. "My magic comes from me and out of this suit. By default, I have to be the guinea pig." She stared at her hand and summoned the sharp, slicing attack spell she'd used only a handful of times—the same one that had almost gutted Romeo in an underground speakeasy for magicals in Montreal. *You gotta love werewolf healing. And practice.*

The yellow light flared to life at the tip of her finger but didn't pierce through the Vátran film. Instead, it flared around the edges of her hand and wavered there, caught inside the breathing suit with her.

"That doesn't look right."

"It's not." Lily hadn't had to focus this hard on directing a relatively simple spell since she'd learned how to conjure flames. *They're all relatively simple compared to the black cloud and my raven totem.* "But magic always finds a way to do what needs to be done." Pressing her lips together, she focused on bringing all the yellow, dangerously sharp light back toward the tip of her finger. It fought her for only a few seconds until it sliced through the film covering her hand. At the last second, she pointed her finger at the ground and released the spell fully. The yellow light struck the soil in front of her and kicked up a spray of dirt and pebbles and a few clumps of dry plant matter. She looked at her companion and blew on the tip of her finger.

He raised his hands. "Easy, killer."

She laughed and studied the split in the film at her fingertip, teased it open a little more, and frowned. "This stuff is way too weird." Thankfully, it peeled off fairly easily once she'd torn the hole large enough to get more than one finger through.

Romeo stared at her as she dragged the Vátran bodysuit away and stepped out of the pile of green film on the ground. "Have you ever watched a snake shed its skin?"

"Not as it's actually doing it, no."

He nodded. "That's exactly what that looked like."

Lily stuck her tongue out at him and uttered a playful hiss. "You're next." She approached him and caught his hand, feeling for the first time the rubbery, slightly sticky substance that had swallowed them as a bright-green bubble and then became an underwater diving suit for land-dwelling magicals. "Crazy." With a grin, she cast the razor spell again and brought the bright yellow light to the tip of her finger. She glanced at him. "Hold still."

"That is a completely unnecessary warning." He swallowed. "I already told you I trust you with my life, right?"

"And that is a completely unnecessary reminder." She brought her glowing yellow finger toward the back of his hand, found the right angle, and slid the light of her spell across the surface of the Vátran film. "It's like cheese shavings."

Romeo chuckled. "What?"

"You know. It's hard to cut a whole block of cheese in half with a butter knife, but you can shave off thin slices if you find the right angle."

"Lily, in no situation whatsoever is that even close to a butter knife."

She shrugged and released his hand. "And I'm not actually a snake." She nodded at the hole in the film on his hand. "You're free. Shed away."

He grimaced when he managed to get two of his other fingers into the hole, and his nostrils flared as he peeled the suit from his body inch by inch. "If we actually find that thing the Royal wants, I know we'll probably have to do this all over again. But honestly..."

"Does it really gross you out that much?"

Romeo yanked the film off his shoulders and drew his hands out as if he were taking off dishwashing gloves. He stepped away from the rubbery substance and wrinkled his nose at it. "My Aunt Kristine paid me five dollars to help her peel the skin off her sunburns during the summer."

"Ew."

"Five dollars a day. I made a pile of money in fourth grade."

Lily laughed and glanced at the piles of Vátran magical residue caught on the pebbles and the dry grasses. The faint green glow they'd held since they'd fitted around their bodies had vanished completely now that the film had served its purpose. "Yeah, that does look like snakeskin." She stooped to gather the sticky, rubbery stuff in her arms and headed toward the cliffs again.

"What are you doing?"

"There's a reason I've never heard of the Vátra," she called over her shoulder.

Romeo glanced at his own pile of frog-people skin. "Yeah, 'cause your mom never told you about them."

"Twenty bucks says that's because even she didn't know they existed."

"Lily, you don't have twenty bucks."

"Twenty gold coins, then. That sounds much cooler anyway." She grinned at him and nodded toward the cliffs.

With a sigh, he scooped up the flopping, jiggling

remains of his suit and joined her at the edge. "Back to the sea, huh?"

"It feels right." They glanced at each other and dumped the remains over the cliff and into the frothing waves below them. The Vátran suits vanished instantly, and she dusted her hands off. "One more thing." She knelt at the cliff's edge and pressed her hand to the hard earth. A blue pulse of light moved from her palm into the dirt, and when she stepped back, a tiny handprint remained.

"Someone's gonna find that easily."

She smiled at him and didn't have to say a word when the blue handprint faded into nothing but soil. "Only me. I'll call it up when we bring the Varelos and need another trip through the cliffs and caves." She turned and looked up on their left toward where they'd parked the Winnie at the side of the road. "Now it's time to do what we do on land."

EIGHT

When Lily pulled her hands apart after about ten minutes of walking, the sheet of faint pink light grew between her palms and she cast the rest of the spell for detecting illusions. The pink light burst from her hands in a huge wave in front of them, making the air a few feet away shimmer against it before the Winnie blinked into existence.

Romeo shook his head and made his way toward the side door. "I'm not even surprised anymore by what you can do with magic." He held the door open for her as she skipped up the two steps into the RV. "But you have a serious knack for judging distances."

She turned and tapped her nose. "And I don't even have to sniff it out."

"Oh, very funny. I have you beat with finding someone else's magic, though."

"Touché." She went up to the front, slid into the passenger seat, and snatched his phone from the center console. "Next step—find the temple of Oneiroi. It can't be that far because we're in Greece."

"That feels like saying every single town in the US has a Burger King."

"Please tell me that's not your temple, Romeo."

"It's someone's." He fell back into the driver's seat beside her and watched her growing frustration as she Googled 'temple of Oneiroi' and couldn't find what she wanted.

"My faith in Wikipedia is nonexistent, now." She looked at him and handed the device over. "We're in need of your skills, I think."

"It only takes a little practice to find what you're actually looking for. Not like I'm gonna compare my ability to research stuff with your spellcasting."

"Hardy har." Lily propped her feet up on the dashboard—which meant she had to slide down in the seat after one of the *Atlantic Maiden's* crew had lost a bet and owed Romeo more legroom in the Winnie. "I'm actually looking forward to seeing this Varelos. Something the Vátra want that badly has to be really cool."

Romeo glanced up at her from his phone as she clasped her hands behind her head. "Really cool and probably really impossible to get if the Royal wants an Optatus witch to retrieve it for him." He clicked through a few more links on his phone and snorted. "You look like me right now. You know that, right?"

She startled, realized her very Romeo-like position, and grinned. "Maybe I'm merely channeling my inner wolf."

"Nice try. It's gonna take a lot more than looking cool."

Lily snorted. "Have you found anything yet?"

"Actually, yeah." With a grin, he turned his phone around to face her and wiggled it. "You didn't expect that answer, did you?"

"You constantly surprise me." She took the device from him and scanned what he'd pulled up. "A temple for Pasithea? She's the goddess of rest and relaxation. How is that the same thing?"

"That's what it is now. Read the rest."

She scanned the article, sliding her finger up the screen over and over while she focused on the text. "Who wrote this?"

"A local. The family's been in the area for a long time, and those are the legends of his ancestors according to the title. But the guy sounds serious about it in his writing."

"A temple that used to be for Oneiroi and now converted into a sacred place to pray to the exact opposite." The young witch glanced through the article one last time, nodded, and handed Romeo his phone again. "It sounds like a good place to hide something."

"Exactly where no one would think to look." Romeo slid his phone into the cupholder in the center console. "Except for us."

"How did you get so good at finding this stuff?"

He shrugged. "I told you, Lil. Practice. I started with finding places that were safe for my dad and I to shift and run around for a weekend. That got fairly hard to do once Charleston started booming as the place for everyone to be."

"I imagine Julian Stephens as the kind of man with a

bumper sticker along the lines of, 'Yanks can't handle the South.'"

Romeo chuckled. "That's close enough."

"So how far away is this temple of Oneiroi?"

"About an hour. Closer than the long-shot shipyards."

Lily slipped her feet off the dash, straightened in the passenger seat, and buckled her seatbelt. "It's a shorter drive. And half an hour across the Mediterranean is a heck of a lot faster than a two-day boat ride."

He strapped himself in and started the engine. "Here's to the fast track with Lily Antony."

"I like the sound of that."

The Winnie's tires crunched over the salt-crusted gravel and back onto E09, headed north for the town of Petas.

WHEN THEY REACHED Petas a little short of an hour later, the sun was almost directly overhead. Romeo eased them into the parking lot of a gas station and pulled the keys out of the ignition. "I think we have to walk from here."

"I like it." Lily unbuckled her seatbelt and stood. "I wouldn't want people driving their cars onto sacred ground in my town, either. What would that be back home? Like the Angel Oak?"

"Yeah, there's special parking. I think they might have closed it off, though, so you can't simply hang out on the tree."

They moved toward the Winnie's side door, and she

turned around to shoot him a surprised glance before she opened the latch. "Seriously?"

"Yep. There was a weird story in the paper a few years ago about someone doing Satanic rituals and making sacrifices right next to the tree. It turns out it was some lady burying her dog or something, but the county apparently wanted to 'do something' about it."

"It might've been an actual witch, too."

He shrugged. "Who knows?" They stepped out into the parking lot, and Romeo locked the side door before he pocketed the keys. "I guess you can't walk through the ruins of Brick House anymore, either. For preservation reasons, I guess."

"That's on one of the plantations in Edisto, right?"

Romeo nodded. "It's a weird contrast, right? We're driving around a country way older than where we're from, and people are still going to the same temples and praying to the same gods, and none of it's closed to major traffic."

"At least not this one. I bet there's something somewhere that's off-limits simply so no one destroys it."

"Maybe."

"Hey." Lily pointed at the convenience store and shrugged. "I would definitely be down for some hunting for magical artifacts fuel. Wanna grab something?"

"Do you even know me?" Romeo spread his arms and smirked.

"Yeah, that's what I thought."

They reached the store and he held the door open for her. The little bell tied to the handle dinged when they stepped inside. "Okay." He rubbed his hands together.

"Brainfood—or magic food, maybe—for a side quest. What's Greece got on the menu?"

"Moussaka to go?" Lily nodded at the hot bar next to the drink coolers.

"I'm so down with a mini buffet in the middle of nowhere." He hurried forward to serve them a few to-go boxes, and Lily scanned the drinks in the row of coolers in case anything stood out. *I haven't had a Red Bull in forever. I can't believe how quickly that dropped off my necessities list.* A shimmering purple can caught her attention and she reached out for the handle of the cooler door. The minute her fingers curled around the metal, a spear of burning agony seared through her chest directly below the hollow of her throat between her collarbones.

She couldn't move and couldn't even cry out as the pain wracked her entire body and arched her back right there in the convenience store. A dark image flashed in her vision—the shape of a bird, its wings outstretched and curling at the tips with black smoke. As quickly as it appeared, the pain vanished.

Her fingers slid from the door handle and she gasped. She stared through the glass and saw nothing on the other side. "What..." Her voice came out sounding like someone was choking her, and she swallowed. A wave of dizziness washed over her, and she pressed her hand against the glass to keep herself from falling forward. *What was that?* She leaned forward and touched her forehead to the cooler door, breathing heavily and hoping something cold on her head would help her think straight.

"All right." Romeo walked toward her with a large to-go box in each hand and looked at each of them with hunger and a little bit of pride in what he'd put together. "We have a box of moussaka and something that looks like build-your-own gyros. That's probably not right, but I'm working with what they have and it's gonna be delicious anyway. Did you find a—Lily?" He set the boxes on a shelf of packaged foods and rushed toward her. "Hey, what happened?" When he caught her shoulders gently, she was shaking.

"I don't know." Lily took a deep breath and pulled her head away from the cooler. "I felt something—"

"I can only assume it was a bad something." He studied her quickly and removed her hand from the cooler door to turn her toward him. "How bad?"

She blinked and had a hard time focusing her vision completely. But she looked at him and was able to center herself when she locked onto those green eyes flecked with gold—and now, serious concern. "Bad. On a scale of one to ten, I'd probably call it a nine-point-seven." The werewolf's brows drew together, and he examined her again. "I'm fine now, I think." Lily rubbed her throat and the top of her chest and found a little relief in the feel of the silver-framed mirror charm on the chain around her neck—her mom's first clue and one of the most powerful magical artifacts Lily had ever used. "It felt like someone was trying to cut into me. Right here." She tapped below her throat. "And...take something out."

He rubbed her arms and glanced around the convenience store. "Okay. Maybe you should lie down for a minute. We can buy food later."

"Romeo, I'm fine." She smiled at him, swallowed painfully, and nodded. "It's gone now."

"Are you sure?"

"Yeah. Let's buy the food for now and work out what's going on later." She tried to smile again, but it felt unnaturally forced. "I still need to eat."

"Right." He hesitated before he released her and turned to retrieve the boxes from the shelf. They paid for the food as quickly as possible and exited to walk toward the Winnie. The little bell jingled again before the door closed behind them.

Outside, under the building heat of a late-summer sun in Greece, Lily closed her eyes and took a deep breath. When she opened them again, she realized how much she didn't want to be inside the Winnie. "How about we sit out here and eat?"

Romeo stopped and shot her a confused look. "Uh, yeah. We can do that. I only..." He looked around them and studied the narrow street before he gestured across it. "Does the bench over there sound good?"

"Yeah." The roads were almost completely empty in the middle of the day, and they crossed the street to an open area too small to be a park but with too many trees and potted plants to merely be a pretty installation. And there were benches. She tried not to drop herself too quickly onto the seat. *I feel like I'm gonna hurt something all over again.*

He sat beside her, opened the boxes of food quietly, and handed her a plastic fork. They took a few minutes to simply eat instead of talking with their meal, and she barely tasted their lunch. Finally, she set the fork down inside the box of moussaka and leaned against the bench. "I definitely feel better now."

Her companion shoveled a huge forkful of lamb into his mouth, chewed quickly, and swallowed. "Better enough to tell me what that was in there?"

"Better enough to say I don't know how it's possible or why it happened. But I think I..." She looked at him and raised her eyebrows. "I think I felt my mom."

NINE

R omeo set his utensils in the box and cleared his throat. "You think you felt her?"

"Yeah. Or at least what she felt. I know, it doesn't even make sense, but that's what I'm going with."

He blinked slowly and exhaled a long, slow breath. "There's a reason you made that connection, Lil. What did you see?"

"Only a shadow-bird. I didn't cast it, but it could've been mine. Could've been hers too." She shrugged and stared at the gravel path at their feet. "I can't really tell the difference unless a raven made of black smoke literally blasts out of my body."

"Okay." He smoothed the dark curls away from his forehead and nodded slowly. "So you can feel your mom's pain now. That's a new one."

"I know. And I don't know how she's still—" She swallowed and shook her head. "I'm not sure I could stay strong through something like this for as long as she has."

Leaning toward her, he bumped her shoulder with his and gave her a small, reassuring smile. "Sure you could. You're her daughter, and you're the one who's gonna find her and get her out of that mess. You can handle anything, Lil."

"I guess I'm gonna hafta handle vicarious torture, too." With a deep breath, she pulled herself deliberately out of her confusion and pointed at the open box on her lap. "Do you want any more of this?"

"I'm good right now. This'll make excellent leftovers, though."

"For sure." She closed the box and rose slowly to her feet. "We can stash the leftovers in the fridge and move up to that temple. And now, we simply have one more reason to get this Varelos as fast as we can and make the deal to get us into Libya."

WITH THE FOOD stored and the Winnie locked again, they made their way along the other side of the small not quite park and past some kind of municipal building toward the hills rising ahead of them on the north side of Petas. A dirt path wound up through the short grass, bushes, and all the cypress trees. The higher they climbed, the thicker the vegetation grew around them.

"Well, this is a nice, private path to a temple," Lily muttered as she trudged ahead of Romeo.

"You know, I like the fact that it makes it harder for people to see us." He pulled his arm away from a particularly prickly bush that stretched its branches over the path. "But it's not so great that we can't see anyone else."

"You're kinda starting to sound like a bodyguard."

He snorted. "If I didn't already know that you don't need anyone to protect you, Lil, I'd go ahead and say I am your bodyguard."

"You wouldn't have been very effective, though, if you couldn't get out of that Vátran dive suit without me."

"And that's why I'm not your bodyguard."

The path became much steeper after that, and she breathed heavily despite knowing she was already in decent shape. "This really looked like nothing more than a hill from where we parked." Romeo merely grunted behind her and didn't say anything.

Ten minutes later, the thick cypresses thinned enough down the path for them to catch a glimpse of white stone and what looked like a manmade wall. "Please tell me this is it." Romeo stopped on the trail, lowered his head, and put both hands on his hips for a little breather. "This hill or mountain or whatever can't be that high, but I'm really feeling it."

"Yeah, me too." She turned to look at him and the sweat stains that darkened the color of his t-shirt in patches. "Are you okay?"

"Yep." He wiped his sweaty forehead with his arm and nodded. "It looks like we made it, anyway."

They hadn't reached the top of the mountain, but the path leveled off and a few moments later, they stepped through the branches thick with leaves and walked into the middle of a decent-sized clearing. In the center was a one-story building, although three of its four sides were open to the outside air. The slanted roof was held up by white pillars on three sides, and the fourth was the only completely solid wall.

"That looks like a temple to me." Lily stepped across the green-brown grass and the piles of larger stones, all of them overgrown with small bushes and weeds. "And someone's obviously come here to do some gardening." She gestured toward the tiny stone pool outside the temple's entrance and to the left, which was ringed with colorful flowers. There was water in it, but it was murky and completely still above the algae-slickened stone beneath it. The pool and the temple looked like the only parts of the clearing that had been touched at all and where the sprouts of weeds and dry grasses and tree branches didn't grow.

"This would probably be more than a one-person job on a regular basis." Romeo stepped past her to peer into the pool. "No one touched the water, though."

"Yeah, I wouldn't either."

He whirled to shoot her a surprised glance. "Why not?"

She gestured at the temple and the entire clearing around them. "We were sent here by the leader of an underwater race to recover his most precious artifact that I assume was stolen and hidden somewhere in or around the temple." She followed that up with a shrug. "It's only a hunch."

The werewolf glanced at the water again, shoved his hands into his pockets, and joined her at the threshold into the temple itself. "So do you think the place might be booby trapped or something?"

Lily licked her lips and cast him a sideways glance. "Did you really say booby trapped?"

Romeo fought not to laugh. "That's what it's called. Okay, fine. Rigged with magic? Warded? Dangerous?"

"Any of those is a thousand times better." The young witch rubbed her hands before she clapped them and kept them pressed together. "It's time to find out." The glowing pink light of her illusion-discovery spell shimmered between her spreading palms, and she jerked her hands away to release a bright flash of pink light. It filled the entire structure from floor to ceiling and illuminated a few lines of glowing silver on the far wall. In a moment, all the light faded and vanished.

With a little chuckle, he scratched the side of his head. "I no sooner feel like I know what your spells are for and you use them in a completely different way."

"How's that?"

"Usually, that pink light's for finding the Winnie after we hide it."

She gestured to the only solid wall in the back. "And it found what someone else left behind too but no wards or rigged magic. And definitely, no booby traps." She snorted and moved forward. He simply shook his head with a smirk and followed her, his hands still thrust deep into the pockets of his jeans.

Lily knelt in front of the back wall where she'd seen the lines of silver light up under her spell. Beside her, centered against the white stone wall, was a square stone platform about two feet tall. Romeo stopped in front of it and nodded. "Do you think something else was stolen from the temple?"

"Maybe. It could've been a statue. Maybe it's only an altar and no one's been here for a while." A soft yellow light flared to life in her palm and she held it up to the wall for another look at the lines she'd seen.

He chuckled. "I'm having flashbacks to the basement of a burned-down house in Colorado and finding hidden messages in the walls."

She moved her hand slowly over the wall's surface and illuminated the silver characters one by one before she moved to the next. "That message was for a few very specific people—Melissa Bore's customers. This one, I think, is meant for anyone who bothers to look a little closer." Once she'd illuminated all three lines of the magical writing on the temple wall, she sat back on her heels and tilted her head. "And it doesn't come with a phone number that I thought was another secret code."

The werewolf leaned down to peer at the writing, then removed his hands from his pockets and squatted beside her. "Does that mean anything to you?"

Lily read the three lines one more time and narrowed her eyes. "Not yet. You know, there's as much magic in the sound of it being cast as there is in the spell itself. I used to think that witches who cast their spells out loud used the actual words only as a crutch, right? Like they needed to actually say it in order for the spells to work at all for them."

"A magical handicap."

She smiled and shook her head. "If that's what you wanna call it. But I met a witch once who could change the intensity and scope of his spells merely by speaking the words differently."

"Like in an accent, or—" Romeo laughed and leaned away from her playful swat, which almost made him fall over.

"No. Like slower or faster or in different pitches. He even played around with putting emphasis on different words of the spell, and it changed the entire intention behind the spell and its effects."

"That's a neat trick."

"It's a powerful trick. I had a feeling that the way he used the sound of his magic made all the difference in the world. That it took a different kind of concentration, you know? I never had the chance to talk to him and ask him myself 'cause he got herded off onto the stage after that to give his speech, and then was all business and—"

"Wait, what?" He smirked. "The way you started that story made me think he already was on stage."

"Nope. This was Alexander Brast showing off before his opening speech at the Magicals with Medicine gala in Boston."

"Lily."

"Yeah."

"You went to a gala with a Massachusetts' Council member?"

Her mouth dropped open in playful surprise, and she looked him with a faint trace of good-natured mockery. "You do know your Council of Magic trivia."

Romeo cleared his throat and looked away from her to stare at the glowing silver writing on the wall. "I looked it up, actually. As much as non-magicals aren't supposed to know, there's a wealth of information on the Internet about our part of this world. It's weirdly accessible."

"And you've thought about what's gonna happen once we rescue my mom and bring her home, huh?" Lily took a deep breath. "You've thought about fighting that fight I promised to drop until we find her."

"All right, don't get too ahead of yourself." He shook his head and tried to wipe the smile off his lips. "The wolfsbane makes a good case. And after all this Black Heron stuff is at least out in the open, if not cleaned up, then yeah." He shot her a sideways glance. "Maybe I'll start working on rearranging the way people think about werewolves. That's not gonna happen anytime soon if we don't get this Varelos for the Royal, though."

She grinned at him and studied his profile for a few more seconds before she nodded and took a deep breath. "You're totally right. So, let's try it out, then. I think a message as totally mundane as that has to have a different meaning when it's said out loud." She narrowed her eyes at the shimmering silver words. "The only trick now is to make sure I don't say it the wrong way."

"Oh, yeah. That's reassuring."

TEN

"'They walked all the way to the top of the hill, and there they saw it, standing still. A pool without a drop to spill. The sound of the dream. They dreamed. This place had everything. From one wish to another's desire, they discovered it.'" Lily tilted her head and stared at the silver words magically etched into the temple wall.

"Yeah, it doesn't make any more sense when you read it out loud." Romeo rubbed his hand over his chin and lowered himself out of the squat beside her. "And judging by the way you're staring at it like it actually blew another hole in Winnie, I assume you're out of ideas."

"Only immediate ideas." She sighed and lowered her hands to her lap as she looked at the vaulted ceiling of the temple. "I have a feeling that the change in the dedication of this temple and the actual meaning of these lines have something to do with each other. Maybe even with the Varelos being here if it even is."

"Okay. That's something we can start with, right?" He

stretched his legs out in front of him until his boots almost touched the wall, then leaned back on his hands. "Right now, this is a temple for Pasithea." He looked at the empty platform on the other side of her and frowned. "You said the goddess of rest and relaxation, right?"

"As far as I know. But if it was a temple for Oneiroi first, like the author of that article and his family have said for generations, that would make some sense, at least. Oneiroi is the god of dreams. Or multiple gods, I think. If we're looking at a main god of dreams, that would be Morpheus, whose most common form is a winged demon. It's kind of the complete opposite."

He shrugged. "Okay, hidden in plain sight is a good option, but actually hiding something out of sight works better, right? Change the name of the place and the reason people come here, and that's generations of magicals who don't know the Varelos is here. If it's even here."

"There's something here. That's for sure." With a nod and one more glance at the words etched into the wall, Lily pushed herself to her feet and dusted her hands off. "I merely need to think about it. That may or may not be easier than trying to solve a puzzle when my hand's about to melt onto a doorknob."

Romeo snorted. "You did work quickly on that one. I still can't believe your mom would set up a ward like that, knowing it would hurt you that much if you took too long." They stepped out of the temple and into the open clearing again. A breeze rustled through the trees around them and brought with it the scent of saltwater and an undertone of olives.

She glanced at the sky and the one cloud she could see before the tall trees blocked everything else from view. "That's probably my fault. I never really learned anything unless it really hurt."

That made him laugh, and he walked across the clearing, shaking his head. He made a massive yawn and growled. "Man. The hike up here took way more out of me than I thought. We got good sleep last night too, didn't we?"

"I definitely did. But yeah, I feel it too." She took a deep breath. "Maybe it's the air up here."

"Maybe constantly moving finally caught up to us." He lowered himself in front of a little mound of dirt just inside the temple clearing, leaned back against it, and sighed. "This is actually really comfortable. Come here."

When she saw him pat the ground next to him, she couldn't stifle her own yawn. "Yeah, that looks good." She went to him, lowered herself to the ground, and snuggled against his side as he slid his arm around her shoulder. They both leaned against the little mound covered in long, wispy grasses studded with tiny white flowers. "Maybe a power nap is exactly what we need to find the answers." She felt his chest rise against her as he took a deep breath, and when she looked at him, his eyes were already closed.

"I was thinking the same..." Romeo's head dropped fully onto the mound of earth, and a snore escaped him.

"Good. Only a little nap." She snuggled closer, pressed her cheek against his chest, and felt it rise and fall beneath her. Her eyes fluttered closed, and she was vaguely aware of a raw, burning itch on both her wrists. *That's not right.*

She forced her eyes open, and the first thing she saw was a pair of glowing yellow eyes staring at her from behind the trees at the edge of the clearing. It was also the last thing she saw before her eyes closed all on their own and she had absolutely no control.

LILY SAT UP WITH A JOLT, startling Romeo where he'd been sleeping beside her. He snorted, uttered a little groan, and lifted his head from the mound of earth behind them. Immediately, he froze. "What's going on?"

They both gaped at the hazy, grayscale fog that slowly filled the clearing. It didn't move like actual fog but more like static on an old TV with a bad signal. Crackling gray lines blinked through the breezeless air, on and off. She rubbed her eyes and could barely feel the pressure of her fingers pressed against her eyelids. It was an incredibly unsatisfying sensation, and she realized the blurriness at the edges of her vision wasn't from sleep. It was simply there and made everything in her peripheral vision fuzzy and smeared-looking.

"I have no idea," she muttered. Then, she remembered the yellow eyes and whipped her head toward the trees on the other side of Romeo. "Did you see anyone follow us? Or maybe smell them?"

"I would've told you if I had." He pushed himself up to sit straight and shook his head a few times. "I think I have something in my eyes."

"There's nothing wrong with your eyes." A woman

stepped from the trees dressed in a long white toga pinned on the shoulder with a copper olive branch. She was barefoot and tall and pitch-black hair fell over her shoulders in waves. "Only with what you choose not to see." She stepped toward them again and the white cloth swirled around her feet and across the overgrown weeds like smoke.

Lily stared at her, not thrown off very much by the odd gray coloring of the woman's skin. She was more focused on her glowing yellow eyes. When she remembered herself and what they were doing at the temple, she took a deep breath and pushed herself to her feet. "Who are you?"

"I am a keeper of the lost things here." The woman spread her arms. "You may call me Morpheus if you need me to have a name."

Romeo realized his mouth had fallen open and he quickly clamped it shut before he stood beside Lily. He stumbled a little under a barrage of dizziness but righted himself and stared at the woman.

"Sorry, Lil," he muttered, leaned toward her, and trying to rub the blurriness out of his eyes again. "I totally didn't even hear her. I should have. I guess I fell asleep first." He shook his head and frowned, wondering why he tried to explain himself when there was another magical standing in front of them. A magical they didn't know and who had snuck up on them and hadn't said anything about what she wanted or why.

"You are still asleep," Morpheus said and her voice echoed a little in the clearing. "And you are also more awake than you may ever be on the other side."

"Okay, I still feel a little foggy." The werewolf shook his head vigorously and gave his cheeks a slightly harder than gentle slap. "But that still didn't make any sense."

"It has been so long since anyone has come to pay tribute to the spirit of this mountain." The woman gestured with a long, slender hand toward the temple across the clearing. "I had to come and see for myself and to know those who would appear wanting something I do not recognize. So I brought you here."

Lily's gaze jerked away toward one of those static gray lines that streaked through the air again. *Focus, Lily. None of this is normal.* "You can see what people want?"

Morpheus' eyes glowed a little brighter, and the smile she gave the young witch was tinged with mournful curiosity. "Most people, yes. Why they climb the mountain. Why they pray at the temple or lay offerings upon the altar. For thousands of years, I've seen what drives them here to this place. And for the last few hundred, none of them have come for me."

"You're..." Lily swallowed. "You're Oneiroi?"

Morpheus merely smiled again and inclined her head. "I would very much like to see what brought you here, Lily."

"Great," Romeo grumbled as he rolled his shoulders, still completely disoriented. "She knows your name."

"A name is a powerful thing." The woman nodded at the unsettled werewolf before she returned her eerily glowing gaze to Lily. "But that is all I see about you. Come." She gestured toward the temple and floated effortlessly toward it, her bare feet silent and fluid over the soil.

Lily definitely noticed that the woman who called herself a god didn't leave any footprints, and the grass beneath her barely moved at all. But she shared a glance with Romeo and nodded toward the temple. "We might as well."

"Sure. It sounds like loads of fun." He grimaced and wrinkled his nose. "I have no idea what I'm saying." They followed Morpheus anyway, despite his gloomy comment.

This time when they approached the temple, the back wall was covered from floor to ceiling with the glowing silver etchings. A mural spanned across the entire surface depicting scenes of sleeping people and flying creatures. Every time Lily tried to focus on a particular figure, it moved. Deer and rabbits darted across the wall. Silver clouds swept in over the mural to hide figures from view. The characters who slept woke when she looked away and closed their eyes again, lying still, when her attention returned to them.

"Do not mind the histories," Morpheus said and stopped in front of the structure. "I am far more interested in yours." She pointed at the stone pool of stagnant water beside the temple, and Lily drifted closer toward it. While she couldn't remember making the decision to walk that way, it seemed she had no choice.

The young witch stood at the edge of the pool and looked at her own reflection. The murky water was now clean and crystal-clear, the bottom of the pool a white so bright it hurt her eyes. But her own reflection shimmered at her on the surface and rippled and distorted her features despite the fact that the water itself never moved.

The woman came to stand on the other side of the pool and caught her gaze reflected in the water. "Perhaps you will show me what brings you."

She heard the words and knew there was something off about them, but she couldn't stop looking at her own reflection. Everything about herself looked fuzzy—off, somehow—and in the next moment, the image that had never quite been of herself changed enough to reflect the image of the one person she'd hoped to see. "Mom..." The word was a whisper through her lips, and she felt Morpheus look up from the pool and at her.

"That is what you see?"

Lily stared at the image of Greta Antony looking back at her, her mom as she had last seen her—smiling, her blonde hair freshly brushed and braided, her cheeks pink and healthy, and the dark circles under her eyes completely gone. In the pool's reflection, her mom raised her arm and pointed at the temple again. 'Read the words.' That was what Greta's image mouthed silently to her daughter. Lily nodded slowly and said, "Yes. I see my mom."

Romeo stopped beside her and gazed into the pool with her. His eyes widened, and his voice was hoarse with fatigue and confusion when he muttered, "How'd the water get so clean?"

Morpheus looked sharply at him, and Lily turned away from the pool to face the temple.

"What do you see?" the woman asked.

The werewolf grimaced awkwardly. "Nothing now."

The self-proclaimed god of dreams looked away from

the pool and grinned at him. "What you want is considerably easier, isn't it?"

Lily barely heard them as she drifted toward the temple and all the moving images that fluttered, floated, and fell into stillness again on the far wall. Her gaze fell to the three lines etched in the same silver glow—the words she'd revealed with her own magic and that the image of her mom had told her to read one more time.

Slowly, the young witch lowered herself to her knees and sat on her heels again. It took her a few seconds to focus on the letters. The gray, staticky streaks constantly interrupted her sight in this strange version of the clearing. But finally, she made them out. "That is completely different," she muttered.

"Huh?" Romeo looked away from the pool and turned toward her. "Oh. Yep. Those are—" He thrust his head forward and widened his eyes. "Are you playin' a movie on that wall or something?" Stepping slowly toward the temple and Lily, his own words echoed to him and pulled him from his daze for a moment. "What am I talking about?"

Lily raised a finger to draw it under the lines of the silver message on the wall and she read it out loud again. "'They walked all the way to the top of the hill, and there they saw it standing. Still a pool without a drop. To drink, to spill the sound of the dream, they dreamed. This place had everything from one wish to another's. Desire. They discovered it.'"

High, tinkling laughter filled the clearing, and a chill ran up her spine. "Wonderful!" Morpheus clapped and grinned. "I have not heard the story spoken as it was meant to be in longer than I care to remember. And I remember everything." Lily looked over her shoulder and thought the woman's smile made her look crazed now rather than from some otherworldly plane.

Still a pool without a drop. She stood quickly and headed directly to the stone pool, passing Romeo but not having the time to explain what she knew that message now meant.

"I'm missing something," he mumbled behind her.

She dropped to her knees again and felt the god's gaze upon her the whole time as she dipped her hand into the still, crystal-clear water. She raised her cupped hand to her lips and took a small sip she didn't even taste. The pool rippled and vanished, and the god of dreams beside her witch hummed in appreciation.

"It's here," Lily whispered and felt it in her bones because her mom had told her to read the words again. And the words said she would find it. "Where is it?" She took a few steps toward the temple and turned again to scan the clearing. "Where's the Varelos?"

Morpheus tilted her head, and her eyes flashed with a deep, amber light in place of the bright yellow. With a sharp whip of her toga, the woman darted across the small space between her and Romeo faster than Lily could see. One slender gray hand shot out to clamp around his throat, although she did not take her gaze off the young witch.

His eyes bulged and he uttered a strangled choke.

"Tell me what you saw!" The woman's shriek shattered the mystical calm of her exterior. Her black hair whipped back from her head and released an even stronger wave of thicker static streaks flashing quicker and quicker across Lily's vision. Romeo clawed at the gray hand that tightened slowly around his throat and his mouth opened and closed without another sound. "If you do not choose the wisest course, little witch, I will keep whatever it is you seek." The woman's voice deepened until it sounded like roaring thunder inside Lily's head. "Choose!"

"No." Lily clapped her hands together and barely felt the impact as she focused her energy and all her spinning thoughts into one single purpose. When she drew her hands apart, the black cloud of her strongest Optatus powers churned between them, flashing with the same silver light as the etched symbols on the wall behind her.

The woman's eyes widened before her lips curled again into a knowing grin. "That's it," she whispered.

She ignored the god and let her power loose in the strange gray version of the temple clearing. With a deafening crack, the black cloud expanded until it covered everything, even the witch who'd summoned it. In the next moment, everything went black, and she couldn't see a thing.

ELEVEN

Lily's eyes snapped open, and she drew in a sharp, shuddering breath. She still knelt on the floor of the temple in front of the wall, and a low hum rose from beside her. When she glanced at the two-foot platform of white stone beside her, she saw the Varelos pulsing with a slow blue light until that faded away completely. Breathing quickly, she extended her hand and took the cold, copper-colored rod in her hand. The inverted U at the tip and its six downward-pointed tines flashed when she righted it, although no sunlight fell within the shadow of the temple's ceiling. She tightened her grasp and looked across the clearing.

Morpheus was gone and so was Romeo.

The young witch jumped to her feet and ran from the temple when a shout of surprise and rage came from the other side of the ring of trees. Romeo flailed against the ground where he'd lain down to rest against the pile of earth. He scrambled to his feet and spun wildly with his fists clenched to search the clearing.

"Romeo."

He whirled toward her, snarled, and his eyes flashing silver. When he recognized her, he exhaled quickly, and the warning glow of his eyes before a shift faded into green. "What the hell was that?"

With a sigh of relief, she slowed her pace toward him and hoped she was right. "We fell asleep. I think that was this place and not the hike." She glanced around the clearing again, but it looked and sounded like a normal space within a ring of trees. "God of dreams, right?"

"That was... You were..." Romeo raised his hand to his neck and rubbed it, entirely confused. "Did we actually have the same dream?"

"If a woman in a toga tried to choke the life out of you, then yeah, I think we did. My best guess is that it was a test." She raised the Varelos, grateful for the solid weight of it and the cool metal in her hand after having not felt much of anything in the dream. "And I'm reasonably sure I passed it."

The werewolf focused on the artifact. "Yeah, that's what it looked like underwater." He narrowed his eyes and frowned. "That sounds like it doesn't make sense. Please tell me I'm making sense."

With a little chuckle, Lily stepped toward him and put a hand on his shoulder. She slid it down his arm, caught his hand, and squeezed it. "Does that feel real?"

He swallowed. "Yup."

"You're making sense. Everything's back to normal now."

"Yeah, whatever that is." He squeezed her hand in return and scanned the clearing again. "No wonder I didn't hear or smell anyone. That...whatever she was wasn't actually here."

"Not unless you can smell spirits and deities." She raised an eyebrow and he shook his head. "She's still here. But we got what we came for." She released his hand, turned from the clearing, and headed back toward the path down the mountain. With a grin, she glanced over her shoulder at him and grinned. "I told you it'd be easy."

Her friend shook his head and tried to clear the shiver that traced down his spine despite the pleasantly warm air. After one more turn to search the clearing, he shot the temple a glare and hurried down the path after her.

BACK INSIDE THE WINNIE, Lily sat on the couch and studied the copper Varelos, turning it in every direction. "Now I really wanna know what this thing is for."

Romeo sat at the small two-person kitchen table beside the couch and shoveled the leftovers from their uncomfortable lunch into his mouth as if he hadn't eaten for two days. He washed it all down by chugging half a bottle of water, then set that on the table and sighed. "I'd say we're probably better off not knowing, but I also know you better than that."

She glanced at him and smirked. "That was definitely a weird way to find a stolen artifact. Or lost or transferred or whatever happened to it. The Royal knew I'm an Optatus witch, and he seemed to think that was especially useful for retrieving this from the temple. Maybe that's true. Maybe it was merely an added bonus. But that woman looked like she wanted to see me use the black cloud."

"Like she wanted to threaten you into it by crushing a werewolf's windpipe?" Romeo cleared his throat and closed the empty to-go boxes. "That seemed a little over the top if you ask me."

"I'm sorry that part happened." She held his gaze until he shrugged and offered her a little smirk.

"It was only a dream, right?"

"Probably. I don't know how many other people would've realized that in the moment. I'm not sure I did. I simply... I don't know. It felt like dreaming. You know, when all the pieces come together and you somehow know what's happening when none of it actually makes sense."

"I don't ever talk like a crazy person in my dreams." He frowned. "As far as I know."

"I think I was supposed to prove something in order to get this." Lily glanced at the Varelos and its shimmering copper surface. One of the tines winked at her in the Winnie's overhead lighting. "I hope you're not mad at me for how I handled the whole...god of dreams' hand around your throat."

"Okay, first of all, I learned a long time ago that it's so incredibly stupid to be mad at someone for something they did in a dream. Granted, that might be a little different when two people share the same dream, but I think it's still a waste of time." He slid out from the booth against the bathroom wall and came to sit beside her on the couch. "So no. I'm not mad at you at all. Honestly, the only thing I thought about was how weird it was that not being able to breathe didn't hurt more." She laughed. "I think you're right about the test part, though. And that most people wouldn't have known it was a dream. Maybe someone else would've called off the mini side-quest to try to save their boyfriend from death by toga lady, but you didn't."

She looked at him slowly and raised an eyebrow. "My boyfriend, huh?"

Romeo shrugged. "I thought I'd throw it out there and see if it sticks."

With a little smile, she leaned toward him and held his gaze. "It might." He laughed and slid his hand up her neck and through the curtain of her blonde hair. When he moved his head and kissed her, she almost dropped the Varelos but set it firmly in her lap. She pulled away and focused on his bright green eyes for a few more seconds. "Yeah, that didn't feel like you're mad at me."

"That's probably because you didn't do anything wrong. I didn't see it as the kinda choice you'd make anyway, Lil. Which was probably the point." He slid his arm around her shoulder, and they both leaned against the couch cushion to gaze at the artifact in her lap. "You didn't choose that over me. You chose to take us both out of that dream with you. The craziest dream ever, I might add."

She nodded, and her next thought made her chuckle

softly before she shared it. "You know, I knew there was a reason I brought you on this Greta Antony hunt with me." He snorted. "You think exactly like I do when it counts."

"Well, hey. But remember I never signed up to be your yes-man."

"Oh, I know. You have different opinions when it counts too." She kissed him quickly on the cheek and returned her full attention to the Varelos. "How about an opinion on what this shiny stick is good for? So far, all it does is—" She sucked in a sharp breath and dropped the rod into her lap again.

"What's wrong?" He glanced at the artifact and then at her grimace of pain. "If you went through all that trouble only for this stupid stick to hurt you, I'm totally fine with tossing the thing out the window and—"

"No. Not the Varelos." Lily rolled up the sleeves of the light cardigan she'd thrown on once they returned to the Winnie and stared at her wrists. "It's these." Raw, bright red lines a few inches thick circled both of her wrists.

"Lily..." He took her hand and her forearm and lifted her wrist gently for a closer look. "When did this happen?"

"Right now, I think." She sucked in another quick breath when he brushed his fingers lightly over the reddened skin and a few tiny beads of blood welled behind his touch. "I think this is like what happened in that convenience store. What I felt."

"This is happening to your mom and now, to you."

She swallowed and forced herself to nod. "That's what it looks like, huh?" A strained chuckle escaped her. "Unless you've tied me up and I somehow never noticed."

He glanced at her and pressed his lips together. "On any other day, I'd find that hilarious."

"I know."

With a deep breath, Romeo brought her hand up to his lips and kissed her palm before he released her and looked at her wrists again. "It's time for healing magic, right?"

"Yeah." Lily wrinkled her nose. "I'm not a hundred percent brushed up on my healing skills. Having Darius around would be extremely helpful right now. Or one of Melissa's potions. We might have to handle this the old-fashioned way and bind it with some antiseptic or something." *Because the Black Heron definitely isn't keeping my mom in a sanitary cage with clean manacles and a daily wash.*

"Does this beast on wheels come with a First Aid kit?"

"Knowing Bentley, it probably has two. I merely haven't needed to look."

"Okay." He stood from the couch and kissed the top of her head. "I'll find something. When that's taken care of, we can get back to our little green friend and hurry across a large body of water." He puffed his cheeks out and shot her a sympathetic frown. "I don't want this to get any worse."

"Me, neither." She smiled. "I'm fine. I can handle a few minutes while you dig through the secret First Aid hiding places." Romeo ran his hand through his dark curls, scratched the back of his head, and cast her another cautious glance. Finally, he nodded and went to go check the bathroom first.

The raw flesh around her wrists had begun to throb now and stung even more when she turned her hands to have a good look at her sudden wounds that weren't really hers at all. *First, I feel them trying to take her magic. Now, I look like I've been suspended by my wrists for days. Hang in there, Mom. Only long enough for me to get you out.*

TWELVE

They pulled out of Petas and headed toward E09 and the cliffs where Watcher the Vátra had left them. Romeo glanced quickly at Lily's lap and frowned at the road. "You're not gonna let go of that until we get there, are you?"

"Nope." She scratched absently at the ace bandages around her wrists, realized what she was doing, and stopped. "We probably shouldn't go to the cliffs first."

"Oh, yeah? Do you plan a few extra stops along the way?"

She rolled her eyes and held back a wry laugh. "Anywhere you want. Or far enough from the sea that Watcher won't sneak up on us again. I intend to find out exactly what this does."

"That wasn't part of the deal, Lil."

"I know. I'm not doing it for the Vátra." She shifted in the passenger seat and turned the Varelos over in her hands again. "It's gotta be insanely powerful for a god or a spirit or whatever Morpheus was to guard it like that. That kinda power can do many things, Romeo. Not all of them are good."

"There's a little part of me that feels like you're kinda talking about yourself."

Lily looked at him and barked a laugh. "Jeeze, it's creepy how well you read my mind." He simply shrugged and stretched his fingers over the steering wheel. "There's something about this Varelos that feels...familiar, somehow. It's dangerous in the wrong hands, right? Exactly like an Optatus' powers. And if that's what helped me snatch this from an actual dream in a temple of the god of dreams, it'll probably help me find out exactly what kind of power I'll hand over to the Vátra with this." She glanced at the copper rod again. "So whenever you feel like stopping and taking a little break, I'll get to work."

"You already have a plan, don't you?"

She smirked. "It's vague and kind of a long shot, but yeah. You could call it a plan."

"Well, we've made it this far on vague and long shots, haven't we?"

"Together, yeah. It seems to be working out rather well."

THEY STOPPED about ten miles from where they tentatively planned to meet Watcher again. She unbuckled her seatbelt and climbed from the passenger seat. "I'll do this outside, I think." She glanced through the windshield at the cypresses lining the road. "Fresh air and enough room to redirect an aftershock if something goes wrong."

Romeo's hand slid off the steering wheel and thumped into his lap. He shifted his entire body toward her in the driver's seat and scowled. "You mean so you don't blow the Winnie up. And me."

She laughed. "That was a joke. I'm using my own magic to determine how this works, not experimenting with someone else's dark magic I should never have been able to touch in the first place."

"That's not even the biggest difference between you and the Black Heron." He sighed and ran a hand through his hair. "Things still blow up sometimes."

"Do you think I'll let that happen?"

"Remember those stories Melissa told us about your mom?" He raised an eyebrow.

Lily opened her mouth to offer a retort or denial, but she closed it again. "Okay, playing around with potions and making your own recipes isn't anything like picking apart the magic that makes up a magical artifact to find out what it does."

"That's not very convincing, Lil." He looked smug. "Or true. I'm fairly sure that's exactly what your mom did when she made her own potions. She probably used her Optatus magic too, whether or not she knew that's what it was." He looked thoughtful. "Huh. Do you think she knows that's what both of you are?"

She pressed her lips together and stared through the windshield at the sprawling mountains in the distance. "I can't even begin to guess what my mom does or doesn't know.

Greta Antony's brain is a locked vault within a maze." Hefting the Varelos in her hands again, she looked down at it and nodded. "I'm sure she knows. Honestly, I have a feeling she found out about it all on her own, maybe even when she was hunting the Black Heron Society, and that she wanted me to discover it the same way. If she'd told me about all this before she disappeared, I'm not sure I would've believed her."

There was a moment of silence between them before Romeo unbuckled his seatbelt, stood, and nodded at the Winnie's side door. "Okay. Get outta here and do whatever it is you have planned with that."

"What?" She chuckled. "What did I say?"

"It's what you didn't say, Lil. I know that look. You won't be able to focus on anything else until you find exactly what you're looking for, so go on. I'll grab a couple of bottles of water and I'll sneak out when you're completely focused and watch you from a few yards away in case you blow something up."

Lily rolled her eyes playfully and turned toward the side door where she paused and cast him a final knowing glance. He propped himself up with a hand on the back of the driver's seat and nodded at her, his expression smug. "Are you sure mind-reading isn't a werewolf thing?"

"Go."

"Yeah, yeah." With a broad grin, she walked down the two stairs and opened the side door. After a deep breath of the fresh sea air, she walked around the front of the RV and headed a few yards inland across the low grass, away from the sea and the cliffs. The last thing she wanted to do was draw any attention from the Vátra, and practicing something like this any closer to the water felt like testing fate.

A small outcropping of dirty-white boulders clumped beneath a copse of cypress trees, which offered enough shade from the sun directly overhead. "Perfect." She held the Varelos down at her side and moved toward them. "There are no buildings around and basically no one driving down the highway. It's as good a place as any."

Once she'd climbed onto the flattest of the boulders and got comfortable enough with her legs crossed beneath her, she grasped the copper rod with both hands and studied it for a little longer. A breeze rustled the leaves overhead, and the sharp tines at the end of the inverted U over the rod's tip flashed at her when the sun snuck through for a few seconds at a time. "What exactly do you do?" She summoned her revealing charm. The yellow light glowed in her palm and she ran her hand up and down the artifact's surface again. Nothing appeared, nothing illuminated, and nothing fought her magic.

Lily took a deep breath and closed her eyes. "Okay. If you won't talk to me with regular spells, we'll try something different." She settled the Varelos over her crossed knees and readied herself to use the black cloud but she didn't have the chance.

There wasn't even enough time to remove her hands from the copper rod to clap them together for her spell. All it took was the thought of summoning her Optatus powers —the magic she'd only begun to understand, even a little—

before the Varelos jolted and a flash of energy raced up her arms, shoulders, neck, and into her head.

Everything around her stopped. The birds that twittered in the trees vanished. The gulls crying overhead and the crash of the waves a few miles away faded into nothing. She felt the warm air blow across her back and knew the sun still shone and the boulders hadn't moved from beneath her, but all she saw now behind her closed eyelids was a blinding white light. It startled her a little when she realized she couldn't have dropped the rod even if she'd wanted to.

But she did hear her own breath, slow and steady and loud as if she'd put earplugs in before this experiment. *What is this?*

'This is the open canvas.' The voice came from everywhere and nowhere, all around her and inside her own mind. It sounded so much like the Vátran Royal's voice—more than one, male and female, multiple tones speaking at exactly the same time.

Okay, I'm gonna take a guess and say I'm talking to a Vátran weapon.

'I am the Varelos,' the voice echoed. *'Not a weapon and not a possession. I am whatever the wielder wishes me to be.'*

What? Lily willed herself not to think of anything at all if the Varelos could actually read her mind. Her breathing hadn't changed, and the energy that surged from the copper rod in her hands still tingled all the way up to her head. *So far so good. No explosions.*

'There could be.'

No. Lily swallowed. *That's not what I want.*

'Indeed. Your focus, Optatus, lies in what you *do* want, does it not? I can see it.'

You can see what I want?

'Would you like to see it as well?'

She didn't have to think the actual word. It was a clear, decisive yes on her part.

The brilliant white light behind her eyes flashed even brighter, and the electric hum flared in her arms and head. More images than she could keep track of burst through her mind—sitting at the kitchen table with her mom, poring over the simple spells she learned for the first time; her attempts to sneak her mom's grimoire from its place on the living-room bookshelf and the way the wards hurled her across the room; the move into their house behind Rainbow Row in Charleston, when Greta's discovery made her famous and rich practically overnight; the first time she sat her daughter down and explained that she'd be overseas for the next two weeks, maybe three, and that she needed to learn how to take care of herself.

When the images stopped cycling, she sat and stared at the same stretch of barren land in Libya that she'd seen in her dream. This was where the Black Heron had taken her mother and where the orange-brown light had shimmered in the air before Greta Antony and her captors disappeared. This was where she had to go.

'You wish to find her,' the Varelos' voice echoed in her head. 'You wish to break the chains binding her to another's ambitions. And yet, Optatus, you have the power to do all this on your own. Why do you seek my aid?'

I didn't. Lily released a deep breath and her heartbeat now echoed as loudly within the silence. *Not on purpose. I only came to find you for someone else.*

'You spoke of the Vátra.'

What will the Royal do with you when I hand you over?

'Whatever the Royal wishes me to do.'

Her grasp tightened on the rod in her hands. *What has he wanted you to do before?*

'I have led the Royal to victory. I have sown chaos and peace. I have united the clans and rent them apart. There is no difference.'

That's not true. She paused and tried to clear her mind so she could ask the right questions if there even were any. *Did the Royal use you to hurt others for that victory?*

'To kill them, yes. Others, he raised to brilliant heights. There is no difference—'

Stop saying that! There is a difference. If he's using you for war, to kill others, to sow chaos, and to tear apart whatever clans you're talking about, there's a big difference. Her pulse pounded in her ears now and all her doubt and confusion rose in her at the words of an inanimate and yet highly magical object. *Will he do it again?*

'Yes. This is the way of the sea. It is the way of the land and the sky. Those who know what they want will do what they must to take it. You know, Optatus. This is your calling as well as mine.'

No. The jolting electricity that raced up and down her arms intensified until it burned. *Not if it destroys people.*

'It always destroys someone.'

That was as much as she could handle. With a shout of

frustration, she dragged her hands away from the Varelos and the vision disappeared. The ocean rumbled in front of her followed by the roar of violent water.

Her eyes snapped open and the only thing she saw was a column of seawater bursting above the rise of the cliffs on the other side of the highway, looming far above the precipice and the Winnie and the outcropping of boulders on which she sat.

"Jeeze!" Romeo jolted where he stood on the grass on this side of the highway. The open bottle of water in his hand splashed all over the dirt, and he spun to gape at the pillar of seawater that rose like a legendary monster. "Lily?"

She exhaled another deep breath and the water dropped and thundered back into the sea as the sounds of everything else around her pounded back into her awareness. The copper Varelos glinted where it lay on her lap, seemingly innocuous and silent until someone knew how to unlock the voice and whatever magical consciousness didn't seem to care one way or the other about who used it to do what.

"Okay..." The werewolf turned and walked toward her again. He frowned at the water bottle he'd been drinking from that was considerably emptier now. "I didn't think you had any ability to make the ocean do what you wanted, but I have to ask."

Lily looked at him and grimaced. "Probably."

"Probably?"

"That was probably me. And this." She glanced meaningfully at the artifact.

"So you worked it out?" He stopped in front of the boulders and handed the other bottle of water to her.

"Kind of. Thanks." She lifted the water toward him before she twisted the cap off and guzzled half of it. "I didn't realize how thirsty I was."

"I feel like you're stalling." He studied her face as he leaned against the closest boulder and looked up at her. "Are you okay?"

"Mostly, yeah. Maybe you should take this for a while." She handed the Varelos to him, and he eyed it like she'd offered him a poisonous snake. "It's not gonna do anything to you, I promise."

"And you know this because?"

"Because you don't know how to use it."

"Huh. Fair enough." He took the lower end of the copper rod.

The minute it left her hand, her fingers felt colder than usual as if she'd taken off a woolen glove she'd worn all day. She flexed her fingers and rubbed her hands to warm them, acutely aware of the bandages around her wrists again, what lay beneath them, and how they'd appeared.

Romeo swung the Varelos from side to side in front of his face and watched it catch the light like sparks. "This is the part where you tell me what happened."

"It talked to me."

He looked at her with wide eyes. "Uh, say that again."

"It talks. Well, not out loud. Only in my head."

With a smirk, he lowered the rod to his side and regarded her quizzically. "Did it tell you what it's for?"

"Basically." Lily took another long drink of water,

screwed the cap on, and climbed down from the top of the flat boulder. "I'm fairly sure you're holding the magical artifact version of me." She dropped to the dry ground beside him, glanced at the Varelos, and looked at his complete confusion.

"I'm gonna put this out there and say that you're definitely more attractive."

She snorted. "The Varelos does whatever its owner wants it to do like a channeled Optatus witch without a conscience or its own life. If you have that, you don't have to worry about an Optatus getting any ideas—no revenge schemes, no one trying to take over and claim your power, and no disobeying orders."

"So, what? This is like the nuclear bomb of magical artifacts?" Romeo held the rod away from him now as far as his arm would reach.

"You could say that. I think that's why it was taken from the Royal, somehow, and why I was able to find it again in that temple as an Optatus."

He frowned at her. "I guess the most powerful kind of witch has a much easier time finding the most powerful magical weapon. Like magnets, right?"

"Yeah. I'm sure that's a big part of why it was taken from the Royal and hidden inside a dream at the temple. Now, we're driving around with it in a Winnebago out in the open for anyone who wants it to come and snatch it."

"When you say it like that, Lil, it sounds bad."

"It is bad." She nodded at the Varelos in his hand. "If anyone finds out we actually have this, we've effectively painted a whole new target on our backs."

"Are you sure you don't wanna take it back right now?" Some of the color had left Romeo's face, although he tried to brush his discomfort off with a smile.

"Nope. Right now, it's much safer for you to hold onto it. At least until I decide exactly how I want to use it."

For a few seconds, he regarded her with a dubious expression. Finally, he swallowed uncomfortably. "You're not gonna give this to the Royal."

"Definitely not." She glanced up and down the highway and nodded at the Winnie. "We should get inside, though. Just in case."

"Yeah, good call." He swung the copper rod down and held it firmly beside his thigh as they rounded the front of the vehicle.

She opened the side door and waited for him to go first, searching the still-empty road for a sign that anyone at all had seen them. *That's all it would take. Only one magical saying they thought they saw the Varelos, and we'd be in a whole different kind of trouble.* She followed him inside quickly, shut the door, and locked it from the inside.

He stood in the center of the living area, held the rod in both hands now, and stared at it. "Do you think it's a good idea for us to keep this?"

"Until we decide what to do with it. It told me that... that the Royal used it to wage war and even commit murder. Something about uniting clans and rending them."

"That seriously wasn't in any way what I expected when we said we'd find it."

"It was definitely a surprise." Lily stepped toward the couch and flopped onto it with a sigh. "We can't simply give it to him. I'm not... Romeo, I absolutely will not be responsible for putting this thing in the hands of any magical who's gonna use it to hurt someone else. I can't."

With a nod, he walked into the small kitchen, opened the long top cabinet above the sink, and slipped the Varelos inside before he shut the door firmly again. "I wouldn't ask you to even if I thought you might." He returned and sat beside her on the couch and leaned forward to rest his forearms on his thighs. "So we'll keep it. If we don't show up at the cliffs to meet Watcher again, that'll call the deal off, I guess. And we'll look for a company or freighter or anyone who can take us to Libya. Hey, we can even drive if we have to. It'll take us a week, maybe ten days, but it's not like we don't know what we're doing on the road."

"Yeah." She nodded. "That is an option."

"But it's not what you wanna do." When she turned to look at him, he studied her intensely with those green eyes for a moment before he straightened on the couch. "What do you wanna do?"

"That artifact can help us get to my mom."

"I dunno, Lil—"

"It showed me where she is. Well, not exactly, but the same place I saw in my dream and the same place I saw in the Black Heron network the last time I used the coin. And I don't want to use that again if I don't have to. We cut it too close last time."

"What happens if you use the Varelos for something like that? Even to find your mom." He ran a hand through his hair and took a deep breath. "There's gotta be some kinda pushback from that, right? Like it feeds your greed or it drains your energy or hurts you somehow. There's no way a magical item like that will simply do whatever a person wants without there being some kinda catch, right?"

Lily shrugged. "It's probably much the same catch as being an Optatus." His eyes widened beneath a raised brow. "The danger is in allowing that power to control everything. What you're willing to do. The things that matter to you. Who you are. Ozias said most Optatus witches went dark because that was what they *wanted*, in the end. They got what they desired with that kind of power, and it turned out to be more than they could handle. Which is probably why there aren't very many left."

"So we use it to find your mom. Get her outta there. Bring her back. And decide what to do with the talking magical stick afterward."

With a snort, she nodded. "My mom would know what to do with it after that. And I think it can show us the quickest way to get to—" A sharp, flaring pain blazed across her face and she reeled sideways on the couch. Her temple banged against the armrest, and her ears roared with surprise and pain before they began to ring. She grimaced and leaned against the armrest, completely dazed.

When her vision focused, Romeo knelt in front of her and touching her head, her shoulder, and her arm. His mouth moved, but she couldn't hear anything over the ringing until it finally faded.

"Hey, say something, Lily. Come on, answer me. Lily?"

"Sorry." She dragged in a breath, and he did the same, his as shaky as hers. "Sorry, I'm okay." She finally managed to get her hands under her and pushed herself up away from the armrest. Her head spun and her cheek stung like she'd spent an hour lying on solid ice.

"What happened?"

"I don't know." She brought a hand up to her cheek and ran her fingers tentatively over it. "I'm not bleeding, am I?"

He examined her, leaning close in concern. "No, but—oh, man."

"What?"

"You...uh..." He stared at her face in disbelief.

"Romeo?"

"You might wanna go look in the mirror."

Lily rose quickly from the couch, which was a bad idea. The sudden dizziness made her stumble, and she managed to clutch Romeo's arm and steady herself.

"Okay, I'll come with you—"

"Nope. It's okay. I'm fine." She took another deep breath and could only look at him for a few seconds at a time. *Why do I feel so humiliated right now?* Her face burned, and it seemed inordinately difficult to focus her vision on any one thing. It took effort but she made it on her own to the tiny bathroom in the Winnebago. When the door slid open, she fumbled in the corner to turn on the light switch, stepped inside, and stared at her reflection in the mirror.

A huge, angry red handprint covered her entire cheek —the same cheek that burned as if someone had slapped her. *But they didn't slap me. They slapped my mom.* Gritting her teeth, Lily turned her head a little to study the mark, which looked like it was rising as a nasty welt on her flesh. After another minute, she left the bathroom and found Romeo standing in the kitchen.

"Try this." He held out a Ziplock bag filled with ice cubes, and she took it to press it gingerly against the side of her face. "I'm so sorry, Lily."

Despite the mingled pain of heat and cold and the burning sting on her cheek, she smiled at him. "You didn't hit me."

"No one hit you."

"Nope. Only my mom." She closed her eyes briefly and made the decision to ignore whatever she felt in her face. "I'm willing to bet it wasn't only a slap with a hand. There was power behind this one."

"There are spells for magical face-slaps, huh?" He folded his arms and pressed his lips together in a disapproving line. "I really shouldn't be surprised anymore."

"I think the Black Heron's running out of ideas. And now they're merely trying everything they can to break her." She couldn't help but pull the bag of ice away and look at it, expecting to see blood there and not at all disappointed when there wasn't any. "We can't take days to drive to Libya. We need the Vátra to take us across."

"Without the Varelos."

"Right. But they don't have to know that's not what we gave them." Lily raised an eyebrow and drew her shoulders down in an effort to relieve the tension there after having been slapped and not slapped by the dark magicals holding her mom prisoner.

"You haven't told me how that's gonna work yet," Romeo said and stepped slowly toward her. He rested his hands gently on her shoulders and rubbed her arms a few times. "But I really like the way you think."

"That's definitely a good thing 'cause you're gonna have to lie to the Vátra with me."

"You know you don't even have to ask."

She smirked. "I didn't." She pulled away from him enough to set the bag of ice down on the counter. Then, she turned back and slid her hands up his chest as he wound his arms around her and pulled her closer.

"Are you sure you're okay?"

"So far, so good." She looked at where her hand rested

over his shirt and chuckled. "I guess we kinda match now, huh?"

"What?" An unsure laugh escaped him, and she gave the center of his chest a few gentle pats.

"Magic's leaving its literal handprint on both of us."

He glanced at his chest and snorted. "Well, mine came from a potions witch drawing a poisoned curse out of my chest. And I'm fairly sure scars stay there forever." The smile wavered on her face as she thought about the day she'd almost lost him to the werewolf packmaster's dark magic in Mexico. "Hey, but just so we're clear, scars are sexy."

A sharp laugh escaped her. "You think so, huh?"

"Totally. I don't think a magical slap on the face is gonna leave a scar, Lil. But if it did..." He shrugged with his arms around her. "It wouldn't change how I feel about you."

"I'm glad we're on the same page." She raised herself on her tiptoes and kissed him while she pressed her palm against the scar on his chest in the exact shape of Melissa Bore's hand. When she pulled away, he was smiling, his eyes still closed, until he finally released her. "Now we only need to figure out how to make the Vátra think we're all on the same page too. At least until they get us to Libya. Today."

"It shouldn't be a problem, right?" Romeo looked calmly at her, waiting to hear what the next part of her plan was. After a moment, he blinked in surprise and turned partially toward the kitchen sink. "Oh. You want me to..." He jerked his thumb behind him.

"Please."

He turned and opened the cabinet again to retrieve the Varelos. Lily pressed her lips together and tried not to laugh when he offered her the copper rod as if he were pledging his allegiance to a monarch and presenting a sword instead. She took it from him and shook her head, and he looked at her with a smirk. "I couldn't help myself."

"Obviously." She lifted the Varelos beneath the overhead lights in the Winnie and turned it a few times. "Now the trick, I guess, is to make sure I can help myself with this. I'm gonna stay inside this time and try again."

"Good idea."

FOURTEEN

Lily opted to sit in the middle of the living area so she could cross her legs again. Romeo lowered himself to the floor in front of her and leaned forward over his lap. "Do you know what this reminds me of?"

"You mean we've actually done something like this before?"

He laughed. "Only the sitting part. Right here, figuring things out."

She nodded. "When we had Rosalía and Felipe."

"Yep. You and that girl spent hours sitting on the floor exactly like this."

"I spent more hours sitting on the floor with my mom, too." She shrugged. "This is a little different, though. We're not working with simple spells and a kid witch who's way more powerful than she knows." He only had to raise an eyebrow to get his point across. "Okay, fine. It's not that different. I'm not a kid, though."

"That's a good thing, Lil." He eyed the Varelos where it

rested across her lap and leaned away a little. "If you actually did have something to do with that whole...water shooting up into the air thing, do I need to sit somewhere else for this?"

"Only if you plan to piss me off when I start talking to this."

"What?"

She chuckled. "I think that's what it was. The Varelos has a weird outlook on death and destruction and how power should be used."

"Like it thinks those are all good things? Maybe you shouldn't do this again."

"No, it merely said there wasn't a difference. Like it...doesn't have a conscience."

"Only a consciousness."

With a shrug, Lily held his gaze and tried not to laugh. Smiling hurt her cheek, which still stung but not nearly as much now. "It probably ends up taking on the values of whoever uses it. And I'm literally only guessing about everything at this point."

"Well, your guesses turn out to be fairly accurate, most of the time. Hey, is this gonna be like you using the heron coin for the network? Do I have to, like...pull you away from it at some point?"

"I don't think so." She glanced down at the rod and shrugged. "But if anything looks off, it couldn't hurt to go ahead and do that anyway."

"Got it." Romeo nodded and chewed on the inside of his cheek. "Reach out and rip the magical weapon out of the Optatus' hands. Totally doable."

"Okay, I'll relax now. I want you to try to do that too, and we'll see what happens. Yeah?"

He raised his hands in compliance and nodded. "I'm relaxed."

She shot him a final knowing glance before she closed her eyes and grasped the Varelos a little tighter in both hands.

Again, all it took was for her to think about casting the black-cloud spell of her Optatus magic, and the buzzing energy erupted from the rod and all the way up into her neck and head. The white light returned, and she was once again seated in the brightness and listening to her own breath and the beating of her heart.

'*What do you wish of me, Optatus?*' All those voices spoke together again in her mind.

I want to know what I have to do to get across the sea as soon as possible.

'*The Vátra offered this to you.*'

In exchange for bringing them the...you, I guess. Will the Royal take anything else in exchange?

'*He will not. And he knows enough to see through the illusion you've considered.*'

Lily paused. *How did you know I—*

'*I see your mind more clearly than you do yourself, Optatus. You wish to deceive the Vátran Royal. A simple deception will not suffice. You must create something for him of your own. Something that is both you and me. A piece of us to satisfy a piece of him. For a time.*'

I don't even... What does that mean?

'Create another. I will help you solidify its temporary purpose but know there is a price.'

She sighed and searched through the bright whiteness but found only that in her vision. *There always is.*

'A piece of yourself. A veil must be lifted from over your eyes in order to pull it down over his. You will see more than you can imagine if you do this.'

But it'll work? And he'll take us across the sea?

'Yes.'

What do I have to do?

There weren't any words in that multi-toned voice to accompany the flash of visions that coursed through Lily's mind in response. The Varelos gave her everything she needed—the spell, the intention, and the piece of herself and of the powerful artifact in her hand. It did not give her an image or an explanation of exactly what that piece of herself was. But when the flood of information behind her eyes ceased, her hold on the rod loosened. The buzzing tingle drained from her head and her arms to settle into the normal sensation of her own skin.

With a deep breath, Lily opened her eyes and grinned at Romeo.

"I'm gonna take that as a sign that whatever you were doing worked."

Slowly, she laid the Varelos on the floor of the Winnie, clasped her hands together, and nodded. "I have the recipe. Now, I gotta put it all together."

"That sounds good." He watched her for a few seconds, then raised his eyebrows. "I honestly expected something weirder to happen. That looked like a few minutes of meditation."

"Yeah, it's kinda like that." She pushed herself to her feet and shook her hands out. "Meditation with a warning."

"Oh, great. Please tell me you don't have to sacrifice anything."

She wrinkled her nose at him and laughed. "Not in the way you're thinking." She clapped and nodded at him. "Now would probably be a good time to stand back."

"Yep." Romeo scrambled quickly to his feet and skirted her to stand beside the kitchen table. "What kinda sacrifice are we talking here?"

"Only the kind that keeps me from seeing everything I need to see." She tilted her head and looked at her hands. "It sounds like a good trade to me." She focused on summoning the black cloud of her Optatus powers and the intention of exactly what she wanted this spell to do.

When she drew her hands apart slowly, the black cloud burst to life between her palms, where it churned and roiled with a low growl. She felt much stronger now and more confident in her ability to control this spell that had given her so much trouble before. *Maybe it has something to do with the Varelos. Maybe I've simply practiced enough. Either way, I got this one.*

Her muscles didn't ache in the same way when she drew her arms out as far as she wanted, thinking about the extra pieces of both her and the Varelos she needed to create. The bright flashes of silver light streaked through the roiling cloud in front of her and flashed off the windshield at the front of the Winnie. She drew her arms fully apart, and the release of the spell felt exactly like when she'd conjured her own raven totem of shadow and smoke. This time, though, instead of a shadow-bird emerging from the black cloud, a long, copper-colored item fell from the space beneath her hands and clattered onto the RV's wooden floor.

The smoke and churning power of her spell dissipated and left a distinctly coppery smell. *Which is probably from that.* She took a few steps back and stared at the exact replica of the Varelos she'd created. "Yeah, it looks like it worked."

Romeo stepped around her and stared at the floor. He glanced from the copper rod she'd held only a few minutes before and the second copper rod he'd watched drop from her spell in midair. "You made a copy."

"Basically."

"But it's not... You didn't make another one, did you?"

Lily turned toward him and grinned. "Come on. Did you think I'd turn myself into a magical-weapon factory and start giving these things out?"

He snorted. "Not really, no. But I have no idea what's going on."

She glanced at each of the rods on the floor and stepped back to retrieve the original. "I made a copy. It's real enough to make the Royal think it's the actual Varelos. Or...it will, at least. I'm not done yet."

The werewolf scratched the side of his head and huffed out a laugh. "Is there anything I can do? Or is it better for me to sit this one out? I have no problem with you doing your thing, Lil. Whatever that is right now."

"You get a front-row seat to an Optatus witch crafting the deception of the century." They both snorted. "This is gonna help us get to my mom and rescue her from whatever hole they've locked her up in again. And it's gonna save many other magicals—on land or underwater or wherever else—from suffering. The Royal's only getting his hands on a mini-powered version of the real one." She wiggled the Varelos a few times and raised her eyebrow. "I got this."

Romeo nodded and dropped onto the couch with a sigh. "I know you do, Lil. Watching you work that spell is seriously cool, by the way."

"Thank you." She picked up the second copper rod, lowered herself to the floor again, and crossed her legs. Carefully, she brought the real Varelos and the copy together until they touched with a metallic clink and crossed them in her lap. "No more talking this time," she told them both. "Only casting spells and moving forward." With a deep breath, she tightened her hold on the artifacts —both of which felt perfectly real—and concentrated on the last part of the magical forgery the Varelos had shown her.

The original released the electric buzz through her right hand and arm first, which made her feel a little off balance. She pressed it down more firmly against the copy and closed her eyes. *A piece of both of us. The veil from over my eyes to pull it down over the Royal's.*

The first thing she felt behind her eyes was a little itch

like she'd blown a flurry of dust into her face and some of it had caught in her lashes. In the next second, the itch had become the same hum of energy as that in her hand and grew stronger until it was harder than she'd expected to not drop both rods and rub her own eyes simply to stop it. She managed to hold tightly to the Varelos and its copy, and faster than she'd imagined, the same force of energy flared to life in her left hand from the forged Varelos she intended to give to the Vátran Royal. The Vátra would take her and Romeo across the Mediterranean and into Libya once she'd delivered it.

After a short while, she knew it was finished. She removed her hands from both rods, which was much easier to do now than it had been the two other times she'd communed with the Varelos. A smile crept slowly across her lips, and she nodded. "Okay."

"Okay?" Romeo moved on the couch beside her. "That's it?"

"Yeah. I did everything the Varelos told me to—" The instant she opened her eyes to look at him and explain what had happened, an agonizingly bright flash of yellow light flared in her vision. This was followed almost instantaneously by a loud crack and an intensely painful flare through her head and in her actual eyes themselves, and she heard herself cry out from somewhere very far away before everything went black.

FIFTEEN

When she came to, Lily realized immediately that she wasn't seated on the Winnie's hard, bamboo floors anymore. She was in her own bed at the back of the RV, her head on the soft pillow, and the comforter pulled up over her. Slowly, she pushed herself up and clenched her eyes shut against the dizziness. Finally, she opened them.

The light was way too bright, and she pressed her palms gently against her eyes as she waited for the glare to subside. It was still there when she opened them again, though—a glowing yellow line in her vision that moved directly out in front of her and disappeared through the wardrobe built into the bedroom wall. She turned her head to look through the bedroom doorway, hoping to see Romeo there. He sighed from somewhere in the front of the RV, but even looking away from the glowing line of yellow light that streaked through her bedroom didn't really make it any dimmer.

Slowly, she turned again to look at the bright light like a glowing cord from her to the wardrobe. "What is that?"

The werewolf bolted up from the couch and came quickly to the bedroom doorway. "Hey. Oh, man. That was nuts." He moved toward the bed, sat beside her, and placed a gentle hand on her back. "Are you okay?"

"Yeah." She offered him a confused smile and tried to focus on him, unable to really take her attention off the yellow streak in front of her. "What happened?"

"I hoped you could tell me. You kinda fell over." He leaned toward her to place a slow, soft kiss on her cheek—the same one that had been struck by the echo of the slap on Greta Antony's face—and released a deep sigh. "Stuff with your mom must be getting really bad if it knocked you out like that."

"I don't..." Lily frowned at the yellow glow, then looked away from it to meet his gaze. "I don't think that had anything to do with my mom, honestly. I think it was the spell."

"With the Varelos?"

"Yeah." She frowned at the bright glow still illuminating her peripheral vision and pointed at the yellow line streaking across the bedroom. "When did that start?"

He turned and glanced at the other side of the bedroom. "What?"

"A bright yellow line shooting into the wardrobe."

When Romeo looked back at her again slowly, his eyes were wide. "I don't see anything bright or yellow or shooting, Lil. Everything looks totally normal to me."

"Really?" He nodded, and she squinted at the constant

streak of light again before she sighed. "Okay, then. Man, it's bright, though. You're not simply messin' with me?"

His brows drew together. "Not about something like that. You sure you're okay? You were out for a while, so I totally get it if—"

"How long's a while?"

"Like three hours." Romeo shrugged. "I couldn't get you to wake up, but other than that, you seemed fine. Now, I'm not so sure."

"I'm totally okay. Minus this weird light." Her gaze darted sideways again and yes, there it was, shining as bright and yellow as ever. "The sun's not gone yet, is it?"

"Nope. It's only like five-thirty or six, I think." He reached into his back pocket to check his phone, then realized he'd left it in the center console up front. "Not that late."

"Even if it was late, I'd still say we need to get back on the road, meet up with Watcher, and get that second Varelos to the Royal. I don't wanna wait any longer than we already have." Her hand raised briefly to her magically slapped cheek again, which still felt tender and tight beneath her fingers. "I don't wanna make my mom wait any longer, either." She tossed the comforter aside and pushed herself to her feet. Romeo was right there when she swayed a little, and she caught his arm for a few seconds of support. "I'm good."

"It's totally okay to take a little breather, Lil." He held the underside of her arm as she took the first few steps away from the bed.

"Not really." She pulled her arm out of his grasp—not

forcefully but enough to let him know she didn't need to be carried anywhere. "We definitely don't have much time left. My mom doesn't have much time left."

"Yeah, and if you don't rest, you can't handle whatever we have to do when we get there. Then we won't do Greta any good at all, at that point."

With a wry laugh, she held onto the doorframe and turned to shoot him a knowing glance. "Either way, I'm still gonna get a little beat up the longer we take to get there. Sure, I could rest a little more, but that's simply more time for those assholes to take their anger out on her. And apparently, on me now, too." She raised both wrists still wrapped in Ace bandages and nodded.

He stared at her for a few seconds, then glanced at the ceiling. "Yeah, okay. Rock and a hard place."

"That would be the amateur version." Lily snorted and headed through the short, narrow hallway through the Winnie. She paused at the fridge, opened it, and selected an apple. When she shut the door again and turned to ask if he wanted anything to eat, the yellow streak of light almost blinded her again. "What—" She clenched her eyes shut and backed up against the fridge.

"Woah. Is this one of those aftershocks, or—"

"I don't know." With a frown, she opened her eyes slowly and adjusted to the glare of the magical yellow cord that had now expanded to stretch from her across the narrow hallway to the other side of the Winnie. "This is..." She raised her hand and waved it a few times in front of the light, which didn't break at all but merely went through her palm. "I don't know what I'm seeing right now."

"I know I'd probably say the same thing"—Romeo scratched the side of his head—"if I could actually see whatever it is."

"Maybe it is left over from that spell. Whatever it is, I can handle it. Come on." She nodded toward the front of the vehicle and moved forward again. The yellow light was so bright, she couldn't not see it, even when it stretched behind her and pointed in the same direction, no matter where she stood. *Ignore it, Lily, and it'll go away.*

She stopped in the middle of the living area and turned, looking for the Varelos. "Where did you—"

"On the couch." He pointed as he came up toward the front of the Winnie. "I couldn't tell which one was which after you— Lily, are you sure you're okay?"

Her eyes narrowed against the yellow glare in the corner of her vision, she turned toward the couch—which made the yellow light far brighter and almost directly in front of her now—and picked up both copper rods. "As sure as I can be right now. I can still walk and talk." She hefted the artifacts and found them exactly the same in her hands. "I can see. mostly. And I feel fine except for this." She aimed one of the rods at the yellow stream of light only she could see and immediately realized which object was in that hand. A buzz of energy flared up her arm and into her neck. "This is the one we want." He took it wordlessly when she held it out to him and put it back in the cabinet over the sink. "This is the one the Royal thinks he wants." She nodded at the replica and took it with her to the passenger seat. "I'm ready when you are."

Romeo rubbed his mouth a few times and finally

joined her in the front. "Okay, I'm not gonna ask again if you're okay."

"I appreciate that." She buckled her seatbelt.

"But if you're not—if something happens—promise me you'll let me know."

Those words made her stop, and she turned to look at him in the driver's seat. His green eyes flecked with gold sparkled at her in the sunlight that streamed in through her window. It wasn't nearly as bright as the somewhat irritating streak she could still barely see from the corner of her eye. "I promise. If anything gets worse, you'll be the first to know."

"Well, I would be anyway." He smirked.

"Fair enough. I promise I'll tell you right away." Lily nodded and stretched her hand out over the huge, plastic center console.

He laced his fingers through hers and gave her hand a gentle squeeze. "Deal." He lifted her hand to his lips to place a quick kiss on the back of it, then let her go and started the engine. "Do you think you can navigate me back to your little blue handprint landmark, or do I need to sniff you out on the cliffs?"

She thumped her head back against the headrest and smiled. "I remember where we need to go. I'll tell you when we're there."

"Awesome."

With the road so empty of other cars, he had no problem pulling the Winnie across the northbound lane and onto the right side of the highway. They began the second leg of their short journey from Petas and Morpheus' temple.

Lily blinked against the sun coming in through her window. *It shouldn't be that bright right now if it's only six.* She opened her purse on the center console—which she hadn't used at all in the last few days—and found out her sunglasses. With those on, she turned and looked out over the Mediterranean on their right and the sun still a few hours away from anything remotely close to sunset. *What?*

Her hands clenched tighter on the armrests when she saw that same streak of yellow light that had blinded her since she came to. Now, it stretched from her body, through the side of the Winnie, and almost directly south-west across the glittering ocean. It didn't dive into the water or arc upward or divert in any way from that single direction, but it did disappear into the horizon when she couldn't see any farther. *Whatever that is, I'll have to let it go for now. It's not like the sunglasses even help.* When she turned to look at Romeo focused intently on the road, she almost said something. *No. It's not bad. Nothing's wrong. It's only residual magic from powerful spellcasting. If it doesn't go away by the time we're in Libya, I'll tell him.*

SIXTEEN

The bright beam from Lily toward the southwest over the sea definitely hadn't gone by the time she recognized the cliffs and told Romeo to pull over twenty minutes later. She kept her sunglasses on, which wasn't all that strange with the sun in the western sky glinting fiercely off the waves of the Mediterranean.

"You're totally sure this is it?" He shoved the Winnie into park and turned the engine off. "These cliffs look exactly like all the others we've driven past all day."

She smirked and stood, passed between the seats, and gestured for him to come with her. "I'm sure." He followed her out of the vehicle now safely parked on the dirt beside the highway, and she led him toward the place where she'd left the beacon spell for herself.

He stood beside her and scanned the ground. "I don't see it."

"Hold your horses, huh?" She clapped and cast her illusion-revealing spell. The pink film of magic spread between her hands, and the blue handprint she'd left in the dirt immediately illuminated. For a minute, the colors all danced together—pink, blue, and yellow because the beam of light the width of her arm still stretched from her all the way across the sea before it vanished in the distance. She glanced at him to double-check. *He definitely would've said something if he could see me giving off a magical tether to something all the way to...who knows where.* She pointed toward her handprint at the edge of the cliff. "Normally, this would've been harder to find." She indicated the protruding section of cliff down which they'd climbed earlier that morning. "But I recognized that part too."

The werewolf followed her pointing finger and snorted. "Something's up with my powers of observation today."

"It's been a weird day." She rubbed his arm and shrugged. "Don't worry about it."

"That's not what I'm worried about." He looked like he was about to ask again if she was okay, but he clenched his jaw instead as if he remembered their deal, and peered over the edge of the cliff. "So how do we get the little green guy to come back?"

"He said he'd be here, right? Or he'd know when we arrived."

"Watcher had better not have followed us again—"

Before he could finish the sentence, a wide, flat green head appeared through the surface of the waves dozens of feet below them, followed by a webbed hand that waved frantically. "Friends return! Excellent, yes? Excellent!"

Romeo shot Lily an exasperated glance, raised his

hand, and waved in return. "We're ready to see the Royal again."

"Then come. Come. I will take you."

"Do we have to...you know." He made a circle with his hands as he shouted over the cliffside. "Go through the whole process all over again?"

Watcher tilted his head and offered them his wide, gummy, sharp-toothed grin. "There is no other way to do a thing that is the only way. Don't take all the time." The creature waved at them again and beckoned them into the water.

"Did that sound like a yes to you?" He wrinkled his nose and turned toward her.

"Basically, yeah."

"Great. Climb down, swim through caves, and be swallowed by more green Vátran airsuit bubbles."

Lily smirked and nudged his arm with the back of her hand. "Do you think you can handle it?"

"At least I'll actually know this time that I'm not being attacked by said Vátran bubble."

"There is that."

"All right. Do you wanna do the honors with this one?" He extended the Varelos replica toward her, which she'd wrapped in an old white t-shirt and tied with hair ties. She'd also pulled a few shoelaces out of a pair of the ugliest sneakers she hadn't worn since high school—but had been allowed to take from her house after her mom disappeared —and made a kind of sling for the item the Vátran Royal so eagerly anticipated.

"Why, thank you." She took the oddly wrapped parcel

and slipped the looped shoelaces over her head and one arm.

Romeo chuckled. "You know, if I saw you from way down the road or something, I'd probably think you had a bow strapped to your back."

"But no arrows." Lily frowned mockingly. "That's really not very prepared, is it?"

"You'd think of something."

"Friends!"

"We're coming," they shouted at the same time. With a snort, he shook his head and headed toward the cliff to climb down for the second time that day. She followed him and hoped that the bright yellow light that constantly pointed away from her wouldn't distract her from doing what had to be done next.

THEIR JOURNEY BELOW THE CLIFFS, through the first cavern, and into the Vátran city somewhere beneath was much the same as the first. Romeo had been right, though. It was far easier to not panic when they knew the giant green bubbles that hurtled toward them from the stone walls were actually there to help them breathe. Once they were fitted again with their slightly glowing, mostly translucent breathing suits, they followed Watcher once again from the glowing coral reef at the tunnel's entrance and into the Vátran city below.

Maybe I shouldn't have taken my sunglasses off before the swim. Lily patted the back pocket of her shorts absently, although the suit made her hand bounce away again.

Romeo caught the movement out of the corner of his eye and sniggered. "There's literally no way to scratch an itch in these things, huh?"

"I'm not trying to scratch—whatever." She rolled her eyes and continued to swim ever deeper, following Watcher as he darted to the iridescent blue domes. Her friend's laughter echoed from his breathing suit like they were talking in a giant, empty building with vaulted ceilings instead of a cavern completely under and filled with seawater. *Not that the sunglasses would help with any of this.* She glanced over her shoulder to where the blazing, ridiculously bright yellow light remained obdurately anchored to her body and stretched toward the surface and through the rock wall and water that lay between her and the beam's intended destination. *And I seriously hope the Royal can't see it, either.*

When they approached the edge of the blue tunnel, Romeo held his hand out toward Watcher and nodded. "Lemme try it on my own, okay? I'm not in the mood to be kicked again."

The green-skinned creature stuck his huge webbed feet out in front of him, glanced at them with wide eyes, and cackled. A few regular bubbles drifted up from his open mouth, but he let the werewolf try on his own this time.

A laugh escaped Lily when her companion tried to torpedo his way through the rubbery wall, his arms stretched above his head and his hands pressed together and pointed forward like the tip of a knife as he kicked furiously and tried to build enough speed. He almost passed through the barrier but either needed more of a head start or the kind of speed they couldn't achieve wearing boots and flats. The barrier gave a little but pushed him away again.

"You would like some help now, I think," the Vátra said through his own laughter. "Tell your friend Watcher."

"Yeah, okay." Romeo rolled his eyes and stared at the impediment as he steeled himself. "Kick away, you little green—"

Watcher's webbed feet slapped against his back and propelled him headfirst through the tunnel wall again. The werewolf's startled shout was cut off the minute he passed through the barrier, and Lily waited for her own push that never came. Instead, Watcher swam slowly past her and extended his webbed hand. "The Varelos travels on your back, Lily friend. I would bring it gently through, yes?"

"Um...okay." She expected her hand to bounce off his, but he wasn't wearing a magical breathing suit that acted like rubber. His green fingers clamped around her own with surprising strength, and he kicked a few times toward the tunnel wall and smiled reassuringly at her. She didn't even have to move her legs to proceed as his kicks moved them quickly enough without her assistance.

Their guide stuck his other hand through the tunnel wall, kicked more powerfully twice with both legs, and penetrated. She was jerked forward, and her hand passed through before the rest of her stuck. Her whole body pressed against the glowing blue as the tunnel refused to give to the rubbery airsuit around her. Watcher's second hand wrapped around her wrist and he gave a mighty tug before she finally broke through the membrane and into the tunnel.

The green-skinned creature caught her and helped her to remain upright despite the slickness of the floor beneath her feet. "That was less awful than the first time." He nodded vigorously.

"Oh, sure." Romeo spread his arms and leaned toward the Vátra. "You couldn't have pulled me through like that?"

Watcher released Lily's arms when she caught her balance and back to face the werewolf who half-frowned, half-smirked at him. "I like kicking you." His short chuckle sounded more like a hiccup before he shrugged and headed off down the tunnel toward the largest blue dome and the Royal's throne room.

Romeo glanced at Lily with wide eyes and shook his head. "I knew it."

"Honestly, if I were him, I'd probably like kicking you too." She chuckled and moved beside him after their green-skinned guide.

"I don't know if that was a compliment or an insult, but I'm really glad you're not him, Lil. Or a Vátra at all."

She pressed her lips together to hold back the laughter and followed the loud slap of their guide's webbed feet down the glistening hall. Once again, the floor flashed its bright hues of orange, pink, and silver. "Me too." On her right, from the corner of her eye, she still saw the brilliant yellow glow of the light that remained doggedly anchored to her and tried to simply ignore it. The glare of it, even where it seared through the glowing blue walls of the tunnel, made her blink far more than normal. *Other than that, I think I'm keeping it together fairly well.*

The bright colors of the shifting floor flashed faster and faster as they approached the entrance to the massive throne room, and she began to wonder how long she could convince herself that everything was fine.

SEVENTEEN

R omeo leaned toward Lily as they entered the throne room behind Watcher. The rubbery airsuits below their shoes squeaked once again over the shifting patterns on the floor. "Does it look like none of these guys have moved since we left?"

She glanced quickly at him and nodded. "I wonder how long they would've waited if we ended up not being able to...uh, complete our side of the deal." *Because we almost decided not to come down here again, didn't we?*

The Royal still lay on the massive lily-pad-shaped cushion on the far side of the huge dome, his bare chest and stomach pulsing with light in pink and orange and yellow. Their guide turned toward his guests and raised a hand to signal for them to wait once more before he approached his sovereign.

The Royal's eyes were closed now, Lily could see that much, and beyond the pulsing light beneath his skin, he didn't move at all.

Watcher stopped a few feet in front of the cushion, directly facing the Royal, and straightened his back. His scrawny green arms hung loosely at his sides and the tips of his webbed fingers brushed against the tattered, seaweed-green fabric of his pants. "Our friends are returning to us now." The creature's voice rose in a warbling echo through the dome. "Our friends are wishing to help Royal now with a most greatest gift. The gift is returning to Royal's loving arms." He extended a hand again to gesture toward the young couple, and the throne room fell completely silent once more.

Without warning, the Royal bolted up from his prone position on the cushion, his eyes still closed, and rose to his feet in one fluid movement without any support whatsoever from his hands as if he were pulled up by a string. His pulsing chest thrust out with what looked like a deep breath, but it remained there, puffed out in front of his shoulders, and he opened his eyes. They glowed again with the same blue of the Vátran domes around them, and he stared ahead, his gaze fixed somewhere beyond the gathering. He didn't look at Watcher even once when he said in the voice that was more than one voice, "You are bringing our friends to us."

Watcher nodded curtly and finally looked at the young couple and waved them forward. The squeaking of their suits on the shimmering floors was the only sound in the throne room and, as before, was a little disconcerting. She was entirely grateful for the fact that she now faced away from the blazing yellow light only she could see. *Other-*

wise, I'd look at that instead of the magical I'm trying to lie to right now.

Their green-skinned guide stepped aside to let them take his place directly in front of the Royal, who stared with unblinking eyes over their heads and across the dome. Lily inclined her head in greeting, and Romeo did the same.

"You have found what we desire," the Royal said without looking at them. "We can feel it again, so close to where it belongs."

"Yes." She nodded and reached up to take hold the end of the faux Varelos strapped onto her back, but her rubber-coated fingers bounced off. "Well, we brought it. I'm not sure—"

"Please turn around, Lily." Finally, the Royal's glowing blue gaze left the opposite side of the throne room and settled directly on her.

For a moment, she felt naked under that gaze. *If I don't play this completely right, he's gonna figure it out. He'll know we're lying.* She lowered her head in acknowledgment and turned slowly. The harsh glare of the yellow beam made her squint, and she blinked furiously against it.

The Royal extended one green-skinned hand—which looked far more like her hands than the other Vátra's—and wrapped long, slender fingers around the rod of the fake Varelos strapped to her back. She actually felt his grasp through the rubbery airsuit, followed by a cold tingle and a small, quick rush of warm air as the Royal pulled the entire thing from within the breathing suit and detached it completely from her. The shoelaces she'd tied together as a strap snapped and slithered down what little space there was between her body and the protective layer. "You may face us, now," said the multi-toned voice, and she turned slowly in compliance. She caught Romeo's tiny frown of concern when their gazes met for only a moment. *Please keep it together.* She wasn't quite sure if she was pleading silently with Romeo or herself or both of them.

With careful, fluid movements, the Royal pinched the residue of the rubbery substance off the shirt-wrapped arti-fact in his hands and peeled it away slowly before he let it fall from his fingers. The film met the floor with a wet, heavy splat, and Lily half expected one of his attendants to rush over to clean it up. No one moved, however.

An agonizing anticipation filled the dome as the Vátra leader pulled away one hair tie after the other from around the old t-shirt. Every hair tie dropped to the floor with a little bounce. Finally, he unrolled the shirt as if moving too quickly would break the precious artifact wrapped inside it and froze. His blue eyes flashed as he stared at the copper rod in his hand before he grasped the fake Varelos with the other had and let the t-shirt fall to the floor on top of the pile of suit residue.

Lily swallowed. *This had better work.*

The pulsing pink light in the Royal's chest pumped faster and faster like a racing heart, although the creature moved as slowly and with as much poise as ever. The throbbing light spread to the rest of his body—his throat, the undersides of his upper arms and forearms, and even the center of his long, lithe thighs. After what seemed like far too long, his glowing blue gaze flickered toward Lily again. "You have returned to us the thing we have most desired for far too long, Lily. Your gift is well received. Thank you."

She was completely surprised to see the Royal bow his hairless head toward her as he bent low at the waist. Beside her and Romeo, Watcher fell flat on his stomach and pressed his face against the throne room floor as his arms reached out toward her. Every other Vátra attendant in the room moved as one and those with nothing in their hands dropped and lay prostrate. Those who held trays or weapons or anything at all merely fell to their knees, but it was enough to send a shiver down her spine. *It worked.* "You're welcome," she said and her own voice sounded steady and sure and maybe even a little full of herself. *At least it's not the opposite.*

The Royal straightened slowly, held the fake Varelos with both hands now, and met her gaze. "We would be very honored indeed to offer you a gift in return. Passage across what you call the Mediterranean Sea, under our very own protection. Would this please you, friend of the Vátra?"

Lily let herself smile a little, and she nodded without breaking from his gaze. "Very much."

"Then it is done." He turned from her to address the very few other Vátra waiting on him in his throne room. "We are setting out to carry our friends through the la-lass. We are wanting every able Vátra who is strong to join us. We are protecting friends of the Vátra. You will be gathering in the time of rising to the surface."

Watcher leapt to his feet and nodded without looking

at his sovereign, closely followed by the other green-skinned creatures who'd knelt or completely prostrated themselves before Lily. Their small, wide-headed friend jumped toward the left side of the dome, stopped, and hurried back toward the young couple on soft, whispering feet. He waited until the Royal had turned away with both hands still firmly clasped around either end of the fake Varelos before he glanced at Lily. "Royal is very pleased," he whispered. "Many Vátra will gather for this diávra. A short journey, yes? But a very great journey when Royal will be coming with us."

Lily startled. "He's—" It felt odd to whisper behind the sovereign's back, but when she glanced at the Royal, the creature had settled onto the massive cushion on the floor, his legs crossed beneath him as he stared at the copper rod in his hands. "He's coming with us?"

"Oh, yes. Very exciting. Good fortune and good protection and good omens for you both, friends. I must go, but do not let yourselves fall over. I will be back very soon." Watcher nodded at them, spun away, and walked as quickly as he could toward the tunnel through which the Royal had originally entered. His huge webbed feet whispered across the floor with very little sound at all. The other Vátra beside the Royal's cushion did very much the same. All of them set their various items down and hurried away in shuffling, gliding, silent runs toward the tunnel after Watcher.

The young couple watched them leave in stunned silence, then looked at each other. "I guess no one's breaking the rules if we're still in here with him, right?"

Romeo nodded sideways at the Royal, who was still completely absorbed in what he thought was his true artifact—his true weapon—safely returned to him by an Optatus witch who didn't know any better. Or who didn't care.

With a tiny shrug, Lily nodded. "I definitely didn't expect him to take us across himself." *Which means that if he finds out that isn't the real Varelos, he won't have to go very far at all to find the witch who has the original.* She widened her eyes at Romeo, grateful that he acted exactly like himself and knowing he thought the same thing.

"Yeah, well..." He forced a smile. "It'll be fun."

EIGHTEEN

They stood there in the silent throne room, alone with the captivated Royal, for possibly another ten minutes before dozens of webbed feet slapped on the tunnel floors and echoed toward them. A stream of Vátra burst from the passage, all of them slowing enough when they entered to completely cut off the sound of their footsteps. Lily lost count of the green-skinned creatures around twenty, but she thought at least twice that many now surrounded her and Romeo in the center of the largest blue dome.

Watcher was among them too. He bobbed his head and flashed his gummy grin when Lily located him among his brethren. The circle of anxiously awaiting Vátra broke quietly and swiftly when the Royal stood and towered above all of them. The fake Varelos swung loosely at his side as he stepped forward across the shimmering floors. The minute he reached the center of the circle and halted only feet away from Lily and Romeo, his subjects shuffled toward each other once more and closed the gap.

He raised his free hand above his head. "We are rising to gather what our friends need from us. Then we shall endure the diávra."

That makes it sound like a chore. Maybe this isn't as easy for them as we thought.

Only about half of the Vátra in the gathered circle held long, copper-colored spears like the two Lily had first assumed were guards. Each of them slammed the butt of their weapon down upon the brilliantly flashing floor, and the domed throne room cracked with the sound. She jumped a little, and Romeo's arm bumped against hers and bounced back when their breathing suits made contact.

The Royal's glowing blue eyes flashed with brilliant intensity, and every stone pool in the throne room began to bubble. In the next moment, columns of water erupted from the pools and raced toward the gathered circle of Vátra and their guests, poured over them, and filled what looked like another bubble that now shimmered around them. This one, however, wouldn't make it any easier for the non-Vátra guests to breathe while they traveled, and Lily was suddenly very grateful for the suits.

When the conjured dome filled completely around them and Lily began to float in so much seawater, the Royal clenched his raised hand into a tight fist, and the entire world jolted.

Nope. Only us.

The bubble with the Vátran leader, almost four dozen small, green-skinned soldiers, and two land-dwelling magicals rocketed from the floor of the throne room and burst straight through the ceiling of the largest blue dome in the underwater city. Her stomach lurched, and if she'd been standing on solid ground at this point, she would have fallen over.

They ascended more quickly than she could follow with her own eyes, although she caught a glimpse of the piercing yellow stream of light bursting away from her toward the surface. She decided to look somewhere else.

The conjured orb rose above the city, which she and Romeo both studied again from beneath their feet before it careened them sideways through the underwater cavern and directly toward the tunnel and the remainder of the creatures' lair.

Lily had to close her eyes as they barreled through the narrowing tunnel of the cavern. It was much bigger than what she and Romeo had swum through to reach the city, but it seemed too small for a traveling group of this size. Luminescent algae, barnacles, coral, and creatures darted past them as they proceeded and their colors flashing brilliantly in an endless dance of light.

"Are you okay?" Romeo asked and lowered his head to catch her attention. The sound of his own voice surprised him. "I didn't think I'd be able to hear anything right now."

"I'm simply trying not to puke in my airsuit." She raised her eyebrows and gave him a weak smile. *That might be the only thing that can make this worse right now.*

The bubble around them filled with light and cast an even starker shadow across the floor of the cavern. The Royal threw his head back and gazed up, followed by every single one of his Vátran followers. Lily and Romeo glanced up as well to the surface of the sea that glistened above them where the sunlight refracted in wavering lights. They continued their headlong ascent for a short while before they jerked sideways through the water. Lily only knew they were moving south again because the flaring yellow cord blazed in the right corner of her vision.

Without any warning at all, before the Royal's ridiculously fast mode of transportation broke the surface, the young couple were both launched into the air again by massive columns of water. This time, however, when they reached the top of the cliffs, they were set down gently and on their feet before the water receded and crashed into the sea.

Lily stumbled forward on the bouncy, rubbery suit that coated the bottom of her flats and tried to stand straight and breathe her stomach back to where it belonged. "You're fine, you're fine," she muttered.

"Woah." Romeo caught his balance and stood beside her, his arms thrust out at his sides before he whirled to stare at the edge of the cliffs. "That whole thing was—"

"Friends!" Watcher called from the water below, and the pair moved cautiously to peer over the edge. "You must choose what you want to bring with you now."

"Um..." She glanced at her companion and frowned. "The whole thing, please. The RV. That's it."

"Yes. Good." He waved quickly at them and vanished under the waves again.

"They're all right there." She stared at the surface of the sea, the cresting waves, and the sprays of saltwater that thundered against the rocks. "And no one would ever see them."

"Yeah, it's a little creepy." Romeo scratched his head and straightened to glance at the Winnie. "So how do you think they'll get an RV down into the water from here?"

She smirked. "In the same way they got us up here, I imagine." The second she said it, two more columns of water erupted from the sea and arched over the cliff toward them. The first crashed over the Winnie, and the second targeted the couple. Before she was pummeled by all that rushing water, she saw the first column recede and the empty, open space of dry land beside the highway where her RV and her home had been. In the next moment, she hurtled over the edge of the cliff again and tumbled over and over in a mass of water and bubbles and flashing sunlight. Romeo shouted something beside her, but she couldn't even hear herself think.

When everything was still again, they floated in the water—under the water—surrounded by the circle of their Vátran escort. Only this time, the circle had grown to accommodate the Winnebago in its center, beside which bobbed the Royal. His glowing blue eyes fell upon Lily again, and he tilted his head. "We thought you might have more than one vessel to accompany you."

The werewolf snorted in his breathing suit. "We travel light, actually."

The Vátra leader glanced at him with languid consideration. "As do we." He raised his clenched fist again, and the massive bubble encompassing a few dozen Vátra, their leader, plus a witch, a werewolf, and their Winnie barreled across the sea however many yards below the surface.

Her stomach churned again, and her eyes watered. That, though, wasn't from the ridiculously fast movement of their entourage. Now, they moved directly across the Mediterranean Sea toward Libya. The achingly bright yellow light that began with Lily and stretched who knew how far seemed to pull them along like a winch on a cable. *Except that I'm the only one who can see it. But at least we're heading in the right direction.*

<hr>

AFTER TWENTY MINUTES of the swift crossing, Lily's stomach finally started to settle. She and Romeo had given up trying to pay attention to the journey. They couldn't see anything but streaming water and a few creatures that flashed by so quickly, they were only a blur. She had pulled her legs up beneath her and crossed them, although there was nothing to sit on, and she watched Romeo study the Vátra all around them.

"These guys have serious dedication," he muttered. "I don't think a single one of them has moved since we started this."

Lily glanced at the Royal, who hovered in the bubble of water only a few feet from the Winnie, his glowing blue eyes now closed and his fist still clenched but now lowered at his side. "I bet it takes a whole lotta concentration to do something like this."

"It makes sense. I wanna know why so many of them

needed to come with us. Don't get me wrong. I like having a little protection on the move. That part's new. And I understand that they want to keep the tall guy safe. But no one's doing anything."

She shook her head and studied the wall of Vátra around them. Each of the shorter, frog-like individuals had turned away from the center of the circle to face outward while their giant underwater bubble hurtled across the sea. "There's so much about these people I don't think we'll ever understand."

"At least we're—"

"The seirí are coming!" The cry rose from a Vátra somewhere behind her, and she turned in the water to see one of the creatures thrust his copper-colored spear above his head. His brethren echoed the call and raised both voices and spears in a wave as they spread on both sides of the one who'd uttered the warning. Everything stopped again, the Vátra froze in their new positions.

"If they are moving as swiftly as us, we are letting them come." The Royal's voice was loud, firm, and sure, although he didn't open his eyes and barely moved at all from his concentrated position.

The other Vátra took up the new cry. "We are facing the seirí. We are letting them come!"

Romeo gawked at the circle of green-skinned creatures around them, none of whom had taken it upon themselves to reassure their temporary passengers. He frowned at Lily. "What the heck is a seirí?"

A flaring orange light that crackled with red streaks illuminated in the water. She wouldn't have known it was coming if she hadn't seen the flaring light reflected in Romeo's eyes and the thin sheen of the breathing suit around him. The glare intensified and grew, and a cracking boom struck the Vátran bubble. A few tiny bubbles rose from the shivering field around them. The Vátra rocked and swayed as one under the force, but the Royal still didn't move. "We are letting them come," he repeated.

Lily whirled in time to see another blazing orange light grow and illuminate the water behind them before it struck the outer wall of the Vátran shield with the same explosive force. "My guess? That's the seirí."

NINETEEN

The young couple both abandoned their easy cross-legged positions that had them effectively seated on nothing in the water. Now, they both faced the back of the traveling Vátran shield, where the orange balls of churning light struck the clearly strong wall with increasing frequency. The next one made the entire bubble around them crackle with a deep, electric blue, and Romeo spread his arms. "Is anyone gonna do anything about this?"

"The seirí assume they still hold what power once belonged to them," the Royal said and his voice echoed around the dome as they sped through the water. "They will discover their folly soon enough."

"I hope that's before they shatter this into a million pieces and pick us all off like fish in a barrel." He grimaced but a trace of humor edged it. "That would be kind of ironic, actually."

Lily studied the Royal and the creature's confident apathy toward whatever reason the seirí were sending an onslaught against them like this. The creature's grip tightened around the fake Varelos in his hand, and she swallowed. *That's why he's so sure. He thinks he can use the Varelos to fight off whatever's attacking us. And then he'll realize it's not working. If the seirí don't get us first, the Royal definitely will after that.* She kicked across the center of the Vátran circle to move a little closer to him. "We can fight them."

"We what?" Romeo turned and gaped at her. "Lily, we don't know what the heck these things are."

"And they're attacking us because the Vátra left their home to take us across the sea." When she met Romeo's gaze, she really hoped he'd pick up on her reasoning. "We don't have many options, Romeo. We're not completely safe yet." She tried to be as inconspicuous as possible when she tilted her head a little toward the Royal. The Vátran leader still hadn't opened his eyes, but she had a feeling he saw far more than most, even with those glowing blue eyes closed.

The werewolf's mouth opened and closed a few times before he nodded slowly. "Right. Yeah. We can fight them." He joined her in front of the Royal while all around them, the Vátran guard remained as still as statues, their skinny arms raised with their spear tips aimed at the surface. "We want to help."

"This is our gift to you, friends of the Vátra." The Royal's eyes finally opened and moved slowly from the young witch to her werewolf friend and back again. "And we will show you what your gift to us truly means."

She tried to summon the red sparks of her favorite

attack spell in her palm, but the Vátran breathing suit only gave her enough room for a few sparks that fizzled slowly and felt a little hotter than they should have. "I'm really not in the habit of letting other people fight for me," she said. "Especially when those people are trying to protect us before we get where we need to be. We'll stand with you, Royal. And the Vátra. But I really can't do anything in this...suit." She gazed at her hand and lowered it. "Can you take us to the surface? If we're up there, I can get out of this to fight and breathe at the same time."

The Vátran leader looked firmly at her and opened his fist enough to clasp it around the other end of the fake Varelos. "That is unnecessary. Your gift was passage. This attack is but a minor obstacle—"

Two massive spheres of orange light burst toward the back of the Vátran shield at the same time, and when they made impact, the force almost tossed Lily through the water and into the Royal himself. His eyes flickered quickly toward the far end of their shield, and she turned. The last attack had definitely blown a hole in whatever this traveling bubble was made of—a large hole with jagged edges that pulsed bright blue in a steady rhythm. The closest Vátra gathered around it and tried to repair the damage with their wide, webbed hands outstretched as they pumped bursts of green light at the shattered shield.

"We are so close to your destination," the Royal told her. "Do you wish to endanger a successful passage?"

"No, I wish to not endanger everyone here because you won't let us help." *And if we can't get these seirí off our backs, he's gonna know that Varelos he's so sure about is actually a dud.*

"This commitment of yours, Lily, we do not understand. There is no reason for a gigni to worry herself over the fate of our—"

A curdling scream came from the Vátra gathered around the hole in the shield. A bright orange hand with disgustingly long nails like talons had reached through the not yet repaired hole and pierced through the chest of the closest Vátra. The poor creature screamed again when the claw jerked away and vanished through the hole. A stream of black-green blood filtered through the water as the dead Vátra fell back among his fellows, all of whom immediately returned to work patching up the hole with their green-lit magic. A few of them released bright-green bursts of their own attacks through the mending breach in the shield. Lily caught a glimpse of something that looked vaguely humanoid as it darted past that hole—bright-orange skin, fiery hair, and eyes that glowed almost as brightly as the yellow cord no one else could see.

Another flare of orange light hurtled toward them and expanded until it pounded against the Vátran shield from a different direction. The traveling bubble around them crackled with electric blue streaks again, and she caught the Royal's gaze. "It looks like they're right on top of us now, and you're losing your own people. You don't have to." Another orange light battered the shield. "Take us up."

The Royal's eyes narrowed at her for a brief second before he tilted his head back and gazed above them. Their escort lurched and changed direction for the surface.

Vátran guards moved like a wave of parting seaweed as the Winnie floated swiftly toward Lily and Romeo. Their leader pointed at his passengers without looking at them, and both the young witch and the werewolf were deposited onto the top of the RV before it rocketed in a sudden ascent. They both threw their arms up over their heads when the Winnie rose toward the surface of the domed shield. The force of the dome pressed down on her, and for a moment, she thought she'd be crushed between it and the roof of her RV. In the next moment she, Romeo, and the top foot of the Winnebago burst through the Vátran dome and out above the surface of the Mediterranean.

"Oh, my God..." She gazed out at the churning water around them and spread her legs to keep her footing on the Winnie's roof as the Royal still hurtled through the water at ridiculous speeds.

All around them, the sea churned with orange light that flashed and pulsated from the darkness below. In moments the seirí surfaced around them and conjured the same orange attacks in their clawed hands.

"What the—" Romeo whirled on the surface of the Winnie and steadied himself to regain his balance before he stared at the few dozen heads that emerged from the water. "I thought mermaids were supposed to be fairly decent to look at. If they even existed."

"I don't think that's what these are." Lily summoned the razor-sharp yellow light at her fingertip and focused it to slice through the second Vátran breathing suit she'd be shedding today. She ripped at the hole and turned toward

Romeo to seize his hand before she made an incision through the film covering his body. "Hurry up and get that thing off. You're right. It's good armor but totally useless for fighting." She peeled the suit hastily from her body but left it pooled around her shoes when she realized it actually helped her keep better footing on the seawater-slickened roof of the RV.

A seirí burst from the water directly in front of them and hurled a crackling orange sphere toward the couple. Lily had barely enough time to deflect it with a warded shield before she delivered her own red sparks with the other hand. The seirí's gold eyes widened before the sparks seared into her face, and the unearthly screech gurgled and died when the creature fell beneath the surface.

"These things are nasty." Her companion turned in a tight circle and left his breathing suit piled around his feet too.

Below them and from all sides, the seirí swarmed toward the Vátran shield that continued its headlong progress toward their destination. "We're almost there." Lily nodded toward the thin stretch of land she could barely see past the glare of the yellow cord that seemed to stretch forever in that direction. *This thing is seriously messing with my ability to focus.* "We only have to hold them off until then and hope the Royal doesn't try to use that Varelos."

"Yeah, it looked like he was really ready to do that." Romeo clenched his hands into fists and scowled at the approaching seirí. "Lil, I don't know how much help I'm gonna be up here."

"Whatever you can do." Two more of the creatures fired their churning orange attacks. Lily deflected one of them and managed to deflect the other to speed back toward its caster's neighbor. The unlucky seirí dropped beneath the waves.

"Jeeze!" Romeo took a step back as one clawed orange hand covered in barnacles darted from the water. The dangerously sharp nails dug into the roof of the Winnie with a screech of ripping metal, and the seirí pulled herself up toward him with only her hands. She snarled and swiped at his legs. "Lily?"

"I'm a little busy." The young witch blasted flaming attack spells at heads of wild, brown-orange hair that swept aggressively toward her above water. When her spells struck, the seirí caught fire as quickly as a pile of kindling, although the flames quenched again the second the creatures dove below.

The werewolf stepped across the Winnie's roof and gaped in disgust at the rest of the seirí's body emerging from the water as she clawed her way toward him—the body of a woman shifted into a tail like he'd expected a mermaid to look, except the end of that tail didn't have a fin. Instead, it grew longer and thinner, with fluttering, sparking fins running along the top and bottom like an eel's tail. "What am I supposed to do?"

Lily turned briefly to see the snarling, screeching creature flip her way toward Romeo. "Get it off!"

He growled and his eyes flashed with silver. "This sucks." Fighting against all his values of not hitting what almost looked like a woman, he stooped forward and swung his fist right into the crawling seirí's jaw. She shrieked and drove a sharpened talon through the pool of peeled-off breathing suit at his feet but he kicked her off. Her body splashed into the sea and was gone, swallowed by the water rushing past them at their top speed and the dozens of other seirí coming to join the fight.

The Vátran dome beneath them shuddered and almost knocked both Lily and Romeo onto their faces. Thankfully, they kept their footing and now, the landmass took on actual shape and form in front of them. A series of bright blue and green flashes came from below the Winnie as the Vátra did what they could to fight the attacking seirí from within the dome of their shield.

"Hey, watch out!" Romeo ducked, and Lily reeled back to barely avoid a mass of sparking brown sludge that hurtled toward them. It landed on the Winnie's roof with a wet splat, immediately followed by smoke and a hiss like acid corroding metal.

With a flick of her hand, her next spell swept the crackling acidic lump off the vehicle. A seirí directly behind them couldn't dive fast enough out of the way. The creature's long, grotesquely orange, eel-like tail flipped above the water before it was pelted by the brown attack from its own people. Lily could've sworn she heard the tail itself scream.

The young witch eliminated as many seirí faces as she could with her hurtling balls of fire and realized that the blue flames were equally as difficult for magical sea creatures to put out as they were for magicals on land. Finally, the speed at which the Vátra transported them began to slow and they approached the dry, dusty coast of Libya.

"This is it," Lily shouted over the cracks and rumbles from the dome below them, punctuated by sirens' shrieks and the constant rush of water as the Vátran transport continued toward the coast.

"There's no way the Royal's gonna beach this whole thing up there, right?" Romeo braced himself for their landing. "That's not gonna be fun for us."

"At this point, I'm not sure he's too concerned about how we get off as long as we're off. Then, he'll try to use the Varelos."

"Do you know that for sure?"

She turned and met his gaze, squinting against the flare of the yellow cord of light that seemed to draw her to some distant destination. "It's a hunch."

TWENTY

The sudden deceleration almost knocked them off the top of the Winnie. Lily snapped the fingers of both hands and cast a binding spell on both her and Romeo. The Vátran dome jerked to a halt in the water, and his body flew forward while the binding spell kept his shoes glued to the roof of the RV. His hands smacked hard on the metal, and he pushed himself to his feet again and shook his head. "Ow."

"Sorry." She grimaced.

"No, it was a good call."

She waited for the Royal to make his next move and deliver them to dry land where they definitely belonged. The seirí swarmed all around them now, and Lily deflected a few more attacks with warded shields. "What's taking him so long? We could've jumped off and swum ashore by now."

"But not with this thing." Romeo pointed at the roof of the Winnie a second before it lurched into the air.

A massive wave thundered behind them, pelted them with seawater, and drenched them completely. The second wave rolled over them and didn't let up. They began to move again and hurtled toward the dry land, but the water in her eyes and pushed down her throat made it impossible to think of how to cast another spell and make sure the Royal didn't drown them in his attempt to get them safely onto land.

The water surged with a roar and the Winnie shuddered beneath them before it thundered onto the sand and immediately retreated. It left a dripping Winnebago Adventurer covered in its own film of Vátran protection, plus two soaked, gasping magicals bound to its roof by Lily's spell. Romeo coughed and pulled a slimy net of seaweed and another drenched plant from his chest. She glanced down and found the peeled remains of her breathing suit completely washed away. His had done the same. She snapped her fingers again to remove the binding spell, and they sat on the roof of the Winnie to slide off it and land in the sand on shaky legs.

"That actually worked." He flicked the water off his hands and into the sand, but it was a pointless gesture. With a scowl, he shook his drenched hair and more seawater off his face.

"We need to get out of here." She nodded at the explosive light display beneath the surface of the water a quarter-mile out to sea. Orange, blue, and green flashes burst like fireworks under the waves, and they could still hear the screeching of the seirí that swarmed in droves toward the

Vátra in open water. "I wanna be as far away as we can get before the Royal realizes what we did."

"Yeah, I'm not gonna argue with you there." Romeo nodded at her and turned toward the Winnie's side door. When he attempted to grasp the handle, his hand slid off and he growled in annoyance. "Come on."

"What's wrong?"

"Okay, I appreciate that they wrapped the adventure-mobile in Vátran plastic wrap too. We won't have to sleep on a waterlogged mattress tonight, but I can't—" He lowered his hand against his thigh. "I can't even open the door."

With a sigh, she summoned the razor-sharp light at the tip of her finger and cut a hole in the Vátran film around the Winnie directly ahead of the handle to the side door. She yanked the door open and tore an even bigger hole in the spongy, rubbery material. "We gotta take all this off first. I don't think we'd get very far with the tires spinning on more rubber."

"I'm on it." He grasped two handfuls of the film around the side door and pulled hard to rip it along the side of the RV and all the way to the rear bumper and tires. Lily did the same on the other side, and they worked as quickly as they could while the sound of the Vátra battling the seirí rose from a short distance beside them in the sea.

They'd almost gotten the thin rubbery coating entirely off the Winnebago, but it wasn't soon enough. A massive flash of blue light—brighter than anything they'd seen so far—spilled from below the surface of the water and rippled out toward the swarms of seirí who still threw everything they had at the Vátra and the Royal within their domed shield. For a few seconds, things seemed to die down. A high shriek rose with renewed force, as did the blasts of crackling orange attacks from the sea creatures who had a beef with the Vátra but didn't care if they caught a witch and a werewolf in their crosshairs, too.

A moment later, a massive pillar of blue light and seawater erupted from the sea, straight into the air, and a monstrous voice roared from beneath the waves. "Optatus!"

"Crap." Lily dropped the piece of film she'd tried to tug down over the Winnie's windshield and pointed at Romeo. "Get in and start her."

"Wait, what?" He sidled toward the driver's door but paused to frown at her. "Lily, let's go."

The surf rising up to meet the beach bubbled with blue light, and the sea foamed with both cresting waves and magic. The first line of Vátra foot soldiers—who only minutes before had dedicated themselves to protecting the young couple—broke through the surface and scrambled up the beach toward them. "We've run out of time, Romeo," Lily shouted. "I'm gonna buy us more. Start the RV!"

His gaze darted behind her, and his eyes widened when he saw the green-skinned creatures bob and weave on their huge, webbed feet. They flurried sprays of wet sand behind them as they made a concerted rush toward the land-dwellers who'd betrayed their sovereign. "Aw, sh —yeah. Yeah, I'm on it." He jerked the driver's door open and climbed behind the wheel.

The sound of the Winnie's engine—thankfully completely dry—turning over and the clap of her hands coming together rose against the tide at the same time. *I hate this.* She focused on her black-cloud spell, summoned her Optatus magic, and let it build between her hands when she slowly drew her palms apart. *The Vátra aren't doing anything wrong. Not like the Black Heron. But I can't let them have that Varelos, and I can't let them stop us.*

The roiling spell of smoke and ash and black, sparking magic churned and grew between her hands. Another line of Vátra soldiers slapped their way up the beach and slowed only a little as the first wave stopped to stare in awe at the Optatus using her powers against her previous allies. Lily had a hard enough time coming to terms with her own conscience in that moment, but then she located Watcher among the second line of green-skinned creatures sent by the Royal to stop her and Romeo. The Vátra who might have almost become their friend stared at her with wide, pained eyes.

"I'm sorry," she whispered, doubtful that he could hear her. But she knew he saw the remorse on her face, even if he couldn't hear it or her words.

A Vátra farther down the line hefted his copper spear and threw it at her. It winked in the setting sunlight, and she had barely enough time to release the full force of her black cloud before the spear would have wreaked its damage. Her spell stopped the flying weapon in its tracks, and the black cloud ballooned in an instant to block her and the Winnebago completely from view. The screams of the Vátra soldiers rose behind her against the crackle and thunderous roar of her Optatus magic, the shriek of all the seirí gathered for battle, and the bellow of multiple voices rising together as one. "You have what is ours, Optatus," the Royal roared. "We will find you!"

Lily raced toward the Winnie's side door and slid a little in the sand. She managed to open it and yanked it shut behind her before she scrambled up the two steps and raced to the front. "Go, go!" Romeo floored the gas pedal the minute she fell into the passenger seat. The Winnie's back tires spat up a wave of wet sand and seawater, and the huge RV fishtailed along the beach and farther inland, away from the Vátra, seirí, and Optatus magic at their backs.

She buckled her seatbelt as they raced across the sand, then erupted into laughter like she'd lost her mind.

"Are you okay?" He tried to frown at her and navigate the Winnie over the sand at the same time.

"No. I'm not okay." She laughed again and buried her face in her hands. "We actually rode across the Mediterranean on top of this thing"—she slapped the armrest—"at top speed and fighting other sea creatures I've never heard of. We escaped them all when the Royal realized what we had done, and the first thing I do is buckle up for safety." A harsh bark of laughter escaped her again, and she covered her face with her hands until the near hysteria settled. He remained silent and gave her the time she needed to pull herself together. Finally, she raised her head, stared out at the red-gold sands all around them and the blazing yellow cord that remained like a pull-rope that stretched in front of them, and thumped her head back against the headrest. "That was awful."

"It was the only choice you had, Lil." He glanced at her and shrugged. "Well, the only choice that didn't involve us being punished for not handing the most powerful magical weapon either one of us has ever seen to an angry sea king. You made the right call."

"I didn't want to do it." Lily closed her eyes and exhaled a huge sigh.

"I know. And I know that makes it harder. They'll be fine." Despite his nod and attempt at a reassuring smile, neither one of them truly believed those words. The black cloud of Lily's Optatus magic wouldn't distinguish between former friend and current foe. The only intention she'd had was to stop anyone and everyone from pursuing them, and any creature unfortunate enough to try fighting through her spell wouldn't make it.

"They trusted us," she whispered.

"I don't think the Royal trusts anyone. Maybe even his own people." Romeo adjusted his grasp on the steering wheel and took a deep breath. "He didn't tell us what we were retrieving for him from that temple. And he called it all a gift. Maybe if he'd said let's make a deal and been upfront with us about everything, I'd feel differently about the guy. And honestly, Lil, I didn't trust any of them."

"Yeah, I know. But I've never had to lie to someone like that for a good reason. I don't like it."

"I don't think anyone does."

TWENTY-ONE

They made their way onto a narrow road an hour later and by then, the sun had gone down and it was completely dark. Romeo pulled onto the side and parked the Winnie. "I think we should call it a night, huh?"

"Probably." Lily tried to look at him, but the infernal yellow light that beamed across the sands made it really hard, especially in the darkness. "This has been one long, crazy day. I'm ready for it to end."

He watched her unbuckle her seatbelt and stand slowly from the passenger seat. With a frown, he did the same and followed her through the Winnie. "Lily."

She paused and for a minute, he didn't think she'd answer. After only a slight hesitation, she turned a little and looked at him over her shoulder. "Yeah?"

"Come here." He opened his arms and stepped toward her. Whatever kind of resistance she carried—whatever bothered her so much that she could barely look at him— fell away when he wound his arms around her and simply held her there in the living area for a minute. Finally, her hands came up to clutch the back of his t-shirt, and she released a huge, shaking breath. "That doesn't sound like it's coming only from lying to a Vátran Royal and escaping an underwater battle." He knew something was really wrong when she didn't even laugh. "Okay, please tell me what's going on."

Lily pulled away enough to look up at him, and her gaze darted to her left toward the couch. "I thought it would've gone away by now."

"What?"

She looked at him and grimaced. "When I passed out after making the copy of the Varelos...something happened. I think that's what the real Varelos meant when it said I had to give up a piece of myself to make it—that I'd remove the veil from over my eyes in order to fool the Royal enough to get us here. That I'd...see more than I could imagine. I definitely didn't expect it to be this."

He frowned and rubbed a hand up and down her back. "What do you see?"

"That glowing yellow cord. The light." She pointed at the blazing trail that now spilled from her side and out through the panel of the RV toward wherever it ended if it even did.

"You saw it when you woke up, didn't you?" Romeo tilted his head and studied her face. Her left eye twitched a little as she turned her head away from the direction in which she'd pointed.

"Yeah. The bright glowing light. I thought it was only there in the bedroom." She held his gaze and shrugged.

"It's followed me the whole time since then like it's attached to me or something."

"Does it...do anything?"

She shook her head. "It always points in the same direction and blinds me in the process. I thought for sure the Royal would see it, but apparently, no one else can."

"Okay." Romeo set his hands on her shoulders and rubbed her arms a few times. "We'll find the answer or a solution. I doubt that you're seeing something for no reason at all and whatever that reason is, we'll find it. Do you have any idea if it's a warning or something helpful?"

"Not really. It's basically pointed in the same direction this whole time. We actually followed it directly across the sea, but I feel like it's too soon to hope that it's anything helpful at all. Look at the heron coin. That's the best way we've come across to find my mom, and it ended up costing good magicals their lives in Greece. Not like we have it anymore, but still."

"All right." He enveloped her in his arms again and rested his chin on the top of her head. "It's probably a good idea not to dwell on that right now, Lil. I'm not saying we forget all about it. We owned up to those mistakes and we made things as right as we could with Ozias and his people. So we learn from it, right?"

"Releasing that black cloud on the Vátra doesn't feel like learning from my mistakes."

The hugs obviously weren't working, so Romeo let her go and took her face in both his hands instead. He leaned down and kissed her softly, long enough to make sure she knew he meant it. Her eyes were closed when he pulled away, but she looked a little less upset. "Come on. Sleep and lying down. Two of my favorite things when I know I'm not feeling up to anything else." That teased a tiny flicker of a smile from her, and he took her hand to lead her toward the bedroom.

"We haven't eaten anything."

He shrugged. "Yeah, something about those seirí made me lose my appetite, I think. I'm happy to make you something, though, if you're hungry."

"I'm not. Sleep and lying down sound about perfect."

"Good." He squeezed her hand and let her step into the bedroom first before he climbed onto the bed after her. "This is all we need to think about right now, okay? We'll tackle the rest tomorrow."

"Okay."

Even as she pressed her back against his chest and laced her fingers through his and he slid his arm around her under the comforter, he had a feeling that all the assurances in the world wouldn't make anything easier for either of them in that moment.

***

EVERY TIME LILY thought she was about to drift off to sleep, the bright, blazing stream of golden light pulsed behind her eyelids and dragged her to full consciousness. She tossed and turned for the next few hours and tried to block it out in different positions, then with a pillow held over her head, and finally with her face shoved into the mattress against the headboard. No matter what she did, it never faded enough for her to sleep.

Finally, she gave up the attempt and slipped quietly out of the bed, leaving Romeo alone in the dark bedroom. She eased the door closed behind her on its tracks and moved across the Winnie to sprawl on the couch.

"Wow," she muttered and stared at the cabinets built overhead. "He's in the bed and I'm on the couch. It's the complete opposite of our first night on the road." A wry chuckle escaped her, and she rubbed her burning, exhausted eyes before she turned deliberately away from the blazing trail of yellow light that pushed through the back of the couch and out of the Winnie across Libya's dry expanse of land. She'd seen it going on forever through the window and even now, as she turned away from it, the infuriating light continued to pulse light behind her eyes. "I'll have no sleep tonight, I guess. So what the heck am I supposed to do?"

She lay there for another half hour and thought she might drift off if she wasn't worried about waking Romeo. That didn't work either and she heaved a weary sigh, pushed herself off the couch, and went to the kitchen counter. Even when she stood on her tiptoes, she couldn't reach the cabinet above the sink. "Romeo and his ridiculously long legs..." That thought made her smirk, and she clambered up onto the counter so she could open the cabinet and remove the real Varelos. "I can't believe this stayed in there through a ridiculously fast passage across the ocean and a sea-creature battle I'm fairly sure only had one winner." She wrinkled her nose at that, shook her head, and climbed carefully down again. "No. I didn't win anything. Fighting with my own conscience and this stupid light"—she swiped an aggravated hand at the beam of yellow, although that did absolutely nothing—"isn't actually a prize."

She took the artifact with her to the couch and slumped onto the cushions. "At least you stayed where we put you," she told the copper rod in her hand. "And maybe you have more answers." She pulled her legs onto the couch and crossed them beneath her before she settled the Varelos across her lap like she had every other time before, closed her eyes, and thought about her Optatus magic.

Once again, that was all she needed before the buzzing, electric energy raced up her hands, through her arms, and into her neck and head. The Winnie and Romeo's snoring from the bedroom faded. Even the yellow light was gone, replaced by the white of her communion with the Varelos. She breathed a sigh of relief. The white light was all-encompassing and bright, but it was the only thing she saw. *At least there's nothing flashing at me right now.*

'*You were warned of what you would see,*' the Varelos' myriad voices told her at once and had obviously already heard her thoughts from the minute she'd made the connection.

No, I wasn't. You said I would see more than I could imagine. That part's true, but you never said exactly what I'd see. This is driving me nuts.

'*This is the price you paid for deceiving the Royal. This*

is what you agreed to do in order to remain the wielder of all this power in your hand.'

Lily swallowed—or at least it felt like she swallowed. *I don't need all your power. I have my own.*

'And yet you know full well that I can help you find what you truly seek. What you desire more than anything in this moment?'

Sleep?

For once, the rod was silent.

I'll take that as a no. Yeah, I already know what I want. So tell me where my mom is. Please.

'I am not an Oracle.'

Oh, come on.

'I do not have the answers, Optatus. Merely the power to help you find them.'

And how am I supposed to find that answer, huh?

'You have two ways to see. One lies in darkness, the other in light. When you choose which way to follow, I will be there to clear everything from your path if that is what you wish.'

When Lily noticed the ache in her temples, she realized she'd clenched her jaw the entire time. *No. I don't want to clear everything from my path. That sounds too much like a dark Optatus. Or the Black Heron. That's not...me.*

'As you wish.' The white light flashed even brighter before she refocused on the darkened Winnebago again, lit only by the never-ending flare of yellow. The buzzing hum of energy in her arms filtered down into the Varelos again, and she held only a copper rod once again.

"Seriously? Did this thing actually kick me out?" Rolling her eyes, Lily dropped the Varelos onto the couch beside her and shook her head. "This whole thing is so much bigger than me. And I don't feel like I know what I'm doing right now." Slowly, she lowered herself onto her side on the couch again, where the cold metal of the Varelos pressed against her back through her shirt. *At least I can feel that. It's good to know this isn't a dream but I still have to find out what that light means.*

Despite the fact that she was finally trying to acknowledge it, the blazing yellow light didn't diminish at all that night. She managed a few snatches of sleep but it was shallow and not much more helpful than if she'd stayed up all night drinking one can of Red Bull after another.

TWENTY-TWO

Romeo leaned against the doorway of the bedroom the next morning, rubbed his face, and blinked through the last of his sleep. "Lily?"

She started on the couch and almost fell off it. "You scared the crap out of me."

"Sorry." He made a massive yawn before he noticed her seated on the couch, leaning over her thighs with her face in her hands. "What's going on?"

"I didn't sleep." Her voice was muffled through her fingers, and she shook her head.

"Really?" When he walked through the Winnie toward her, he noticed the Varelos lying on the couch behind her and stopped. "You didn't sleep 'cause you were up all night with that, or was it something else?"

"What?" She looked at him, dark circles under her eyes, and squinted in an effort to focus. He nodded at the copper rod almost stuffed between the couch cushions, and she glanced down before she realized what he meant. "Oh.

No, I didn't use that all night. I couldn't sleep in bed, so I came out here and thought I'd ask it a few questions."

"Did you get any answers?" He sat beside her on the couch, hauled the Varelos from between the cushions, and lifted it over both their heads before he placed it on the floor.

"Oh, yeah, I got answers. None of them were helpful, though."

"The most powerful magical artifact-slash-weapon wasn't helpful."

Lily gave him an exasperated look, although it had definitely lost its effectiveness under her exhaustion. "Apparently, I didn't ask the right questions. Or maybe I simply don't want the right things. That hunk of metal told me it wasn't an Oracle, so it couldn't tell me where they're keeping my mom now. But it did make the oh so generous offer to basically obliterate everyone in my way with a magical machete if that was what I wanted."

Romeo's brows flickered together, and he scratched the side of his face. "Was that a literal offer?"

"No, Romeo, it wasn't literal. The artifact said it would be there to clear everything from my path—if that's what I wanted—after I chose how I wanted to see."

"That doesn't make much sense."

She shook her head. "It said something about seeing two ways. Light and dark. Obviously, that's talking about my magic. Do I wanna keep my soul, or do I wanna give in and let the Varelos do all the dirty work for me simply to make my life easier?"

"Okay. Normally, I'd say this is something a good cup

of coffee can fix. But seeing as you didn't sleep, Lil, I'll chalk it up to that. It's hard to not let it get to you. I know. But you gotta try."

Slowly, she looked at him and studied his green eyes flecked with gold. "You're right." She caught his hand and laced their fingers together. "I'm sorry. I'm only... I guess I don't do well on no sleep."

"No sleep. A stream of light that you apparently see all the time. A massive battle in the middle of the ocean between two races who really have nothing to do with us until they tried to punish you for not giving them the dangerous magical weapon we took from the god of dreams." He squeezed her hand. "Lily, you don't have anything to be sorry for. Seriously. You're handling this way better than anyone else. Definitely better than I would. I'm constantly amazed by that. Now, try to breathe through it, okay? We'll find the answers we need, and I'm here with you through all of it. I promise."

She released a shaky sigh. "Yeah, when you put it that way, it does sound impossibly overwhelming." That made him smirk, and she couldn't help but return it. "I want this to be over. I want to find her and stop the Black Heron from getting anything else they want. There's way too much on the line to let them get away with what they've already done and what they plan to do. No one should have that much magic at their fingertips, especially when they're only gonna use it to constantly destroy everything that keeps the magical world safe."

"That's a huge responsibility to put on your shoulders."

Lily chewed on the inside of her lower lip and stared at

the floor. "I originally thought we would simply find my mom. We could prove to the world that she's not dead and keep that witch guy in Charleston from trying to kill me."

"And it turned out to be far more than that. I know."

A humorless laugh escaped her. "What did my mom do to them to make them so dedicated to destroying her?"

"I think it's what she didn't do, Lil." She looked at him again, and Romeo lifted her hand to press it between both of his. "She wouldn't give in. Your mom didn't give up and let them take whatever they wanted from her—her magic. And jeez, whether they know it or not, they'd pull Optatus magic out of her. She can't give up. If they add that to the pot, I don't know if anyone will be able to stop them." She closed her eyes. "Hey, look at me." When she did, he was studying her intently and with real compassion, his brows raised in concern and determination at the same time. "But you can."

"You say that like you can see the future."

"I can with you."

Lily shuddered.

"I've always known what you can do. Okay, not specifically. Not all the spells and the black cloud and the shadow-bird. But for as long as I've known you, if you wanted to do something—really wanted to do it—you did it. You always find a way. And anyone who tries to stop you has no idea who they're messing with. Being an Optatus doesn't change who you are." He lifted her hand and pressed it against his chest. "It doesn't change what we've been through in the last few months. Or the fact that every single time I start to think we've reached a dead end or a wall we can't get through or over or around, you find a way to do it anyway. It doesn't change how much I love you, Lily. So I'm not gonna let you talk yourself out of being who you are. Got it?"

Despite how exhausted she was, the young witch found her nose burning and a few tears made her vision shimmer. But she managed to keep them there and prevent them from spilling onto her cheeks. "That was one of the best speeches I've ever heard."

He laughed and glanced at the ceiling. "Well, it kinda came out."

"I'm serious, though. Hey." She pressed on his chest where he held her hand there, right over the handprint scar left from the night she'd fed him poison to save his life. Romeo looked at her and his smile was both uplifting and loving. "Thank you. That's what I needed to hear. I can't see the future like you can." That made them both smile a little. "But I'm not giving up. I'm starting to think I might have by now if you weren't here with me."

"We're on the same page with that one."

She cupped his cheek with her free hand, leaned toward him on the couch, and kissed him. His long, deep breath only made her inch closer, and she held his face in both hands now, her lips on his as she crawled up into his lap. He slid his arms around her and held her close for a long moment until she pulled back to look at him. "I love you too."

He grinned. "You know, that's the second time we've said that to each other, and I almost thought you hadn't heard me."

"I'm tired and frustrated and constantly see a glowing line of light that never goes away, Romeo. I definitely heard you." She kissed him again quickly, slid out of his lap, and stood. "So, I obviously won't have any sleep, and we can't get anything done sitting here in the middle of nowhere. We might as well get some coffee in and food of some kind. Then, we'll decide what the next move should be."

With a tiny smile, Romeo rose from the couch and tucked her blonde hair behind her ear. "Coffee is the least I can do."

"And at the same time, it's also a big deal."

He laughed and headed toward the kitchen counter to pull out the French press and their almost empty supply of coffee grounds. "If this lasts us long enough to find your mom, I'd say we've done something right."

Lily passed him, opened the fridge, and squinted against the light that shined over their almost empty shelves. "We've done any number of things right. Keeping that coffee from running out is definitely one of them." She pulled out the last package of dolmades they'd picked up in Greece and closed the fridge again, fighting through the dizziness of not having slept. *Now we only need to keep that up and not do anything wrong. We don't have room for mistakes anymore. Neither does my mom.*

TWENTY-THREE

Romeo placed their clean breakfast dishes on the drying rack beside the sink and returned to the table. He glanced at the coffee cup nestled between Lily's hands, then looked at his own. "Do you want the rest of mine?"

"Huh?"

"My coffee."

"Oh." She frowned and eyed both their cups for a few seconds. "Are you not gonna finish it?"

"I had a full night of sleep, Lil. I can sacrifice two-thirds of a cup of coffee."

She smiled at him and stretched across the table for his mug. "Thank you very much." Holding his gaze, she brought it to her lips and took a huge gulp. "It definitely helps."

"Good." He rapped his knuckles on the table and headed toward the front. "Next thing on the magical-adventure to-do list is to find out where the heck we are and where we'll go next."

"We'd better be in Libya," she muttered before she took another sip of coffee. "That's as far as I saw the last time I used the heron coin." Romeo paused behind the center console, stretched to retrieve his phone, and brought it back with him. "Beyond that, I have no clue. The Varelos isn't really helping, either."

"We don't need no stinkin' Varelos."

She snorted. "True. I don't think anyone needs it. Who even creates something like that in the first place?"

Romeo slid into the booth across from her and eased his legs around the pot of wolfsbane they still hadn't moved from its extremely inconvenient location. "Probably someone who thought they needed it and that it would help them somehow."

"I can't imagine making something that powerful for myself to use. Okay, yeah, it's more or less an Optatus' magic funneled into a single artifact that kinda has a mind of its own, but I was born with my magic. I wouldn't try to give it to anyone." Lily glanced at him as he scrolled through something on his phone and raised her eyebrows. "What if an Optatus made it? Like they tried to funnel their magic into an item someone else could use?"

His gaze flickered briefly to her before he resumed his lightspeed research. "Why would someone want to do that?"

"Hey, I'd do it if it was the only way to help you out of some kind of impossible situation."

He scowled, took a deep breath, and lowered his phone to look firmly at her. "Don't."

"What? Don't turn my Optatus powers into a weapon to save you?"

The werewolf's eyes narrowed above a hesitant smile. "If you ever need to save me, do it with your magic and when it's still attached to you. You did it once, and you could do it again. But... I don't know if any one person's worth the kinda trouble that can cause." He nodded at the Varelos on the floor by the couch. "Not even me, probably."

"That's totally not true." When he replied with a skeptical frown, she decided to let it pass. "I won't do it, Romeo. This is a hypothetical situation, and I wouldn't even know how to do it in the first place. It simply...feels like it would be easier to deal with having that around if I understood why it exists."

Romeo's frown disappeared, replaced by a gentle smile. "That's kinda like trying to find the meaning of life, don't you think?"

"And people have looked for that answer since the beginning of people." She lifted the coffee cup to her lips and drank again. *You sound like you're losing it, Lily. Let him do his thing. You're not very helpful after a night of no sleep at all.*

"Okay. I found where we are. Right outside Bin Jawad and definitely in Libya."

"Good."

"Is there anything else you can remember about your

dream? Or seeing your mom in the network? Landmarks, roads, signs like you saw for Oitylo?"

Lily stared at the table as she recalled the dream. "Nope. Only that they pulled off the road in the middle of nowhere." She turned in the booth enough to look out the windows at the red, dusty, dry land that spread all around them and back toward the Mediterranean. "It basically looked much like where we are now, actually."

"Huh. So they could be super-close."

"I don't think so."

He frowned at his phone. "You'd know if we were close."

"Right. We can count on that, right? It makes sense. If I am blasted in the chest and have manacle burns"—she lifted her wrists—"and am slapped in the face by a hand that's not there, I'd feel it if we were at the right place."

"Probably." He didn't look at her.

Lily straightened and took a deep breath. "I could try to find her with my raven totem."

"Are you sure?"

"Not really, but it's worth a try. If she learned how to send hers halfway across the world to look out for me, so can I. Especially now that we're in the same country."

For a minute, she thought he would tell her to forget it judging by the way he stared at her. "Okay." Romeo nodded. "But keep it to one attempt for now, yeah? Remember the night you cast that spell over and over for hours? Before you activated the heron coin."

"Yeah, I know. That was a little excessive."

"You couldn't really walk straight, Lil. And that was on eight hours of sleep the night before."

She nodded in acknowledgment. "Got it. I'll only try once. And if it doesn't work, we'll think of something else."

He pressed his lips together and almost told her of the other option they did still have, then decided against it. "Sounds good."

"Okay." She pushed herself up from the table and slid out of the booth. "I'll go outside and get some fresh air while I try to focus on this." She headed across the Winnie toward the side door and stopped to look at him over her shoulder. "It probably won't take me very long, but you can come with me if you want to."

"I thought you'd never ask." With a little smirk, he lifted his leg over the pot of wolfsbane under the table and stood.

"Really?" Lily smirked. "I think it's fairly obvious by now that—" A massive crack like thunder pealed in her head and lasted longer than thunder ever should. Everything around her—the Winnie, Romeo, and even that blinding trail of yellow light always pointing in the same direction—vanished, replaced only by a sudden blackness and a pain unlike anything she'd ever known. Every muscle in her body tensed up, quivering, and she couldn't even cry out as the thunder echoed over and over through her head, beating her awareness down into pain and noise and darkness. Maybe she did scream something. She thought she heard Romeo shout her name, but then there was nothing at all.

"Lily!" Romeo's phone clattered to the floor as he leapt across the Winnebago toward her. He wasn't fast enough to keep her from crumpling in front of him like a puppet cut from its strings, and by the time he skidded on his knees next to her, she was convulsing on the floor. Her eyes rolled all the way back in her head to show nothing but the whites, and a terrifying gurgle came from her throat. "Hey, Lily. Can you hear me?" It was a ridiculous question, he knew, but it was the only thing he could think of as he wound his arms around her and tried to hold her still. His first instinct was to try to keep her from flailing and hurting herself more than whatever was already hurting her.

The convulsions ceased as quickly as they had seized control of her, and it was even more terrifying to hold her now that she lay completely limp and unresponsive. "Lily?" He rubbed her shoulders despite wanting to shake her, but she was out cold. "Oh, man..." A thin stream of blood trickled from her nose, and he felt something warm and wet drip on his forearm before he realized she was bleeding from her ears too. "No, no, no." He bent his head toward her open mouth and felt her slow, steady breath against his ear, at least.

In one fluid motion, he scooped her up and carried her to the front of the RV, where he set her as gently as he could in the passenger seat. He strapped her in, ran to grab his phone, and discovered that the closest hospital in Libya was five hours away. "Okay. Hold on, Lil." He slid behind the wheel, started the engine, and strapped his seatbelt on hurriedly before he floored the gas again. "Don't give up on me. We'll fix this."

The Winnie rocked dangerously over a skidding spray of sand and small pebbles, and he almost didn't manage to straighten it out on the road once the tires made contact with the asphalt. Fortunately, he did, and he didn't even look at the speedometer as he barreled toward the hospital in Zliten.

If she were conscious, she would have told him he was moving in the same direction as the bright yellow cord of magical light stretching from her body that only she could see.

TWENTY-FOUR

Lily gasped and bolted fully upright in the passenger seat. "Mom!"

"What—" Romeo jumped in driver's seat beside her and his hands jerked on the wheel and veered them into the other lane at the same moment that a small gray sedan raced past them. The driver held their horn down indignantly, and Romeo corrected with barely enough time to avoid a head-on collision that would have been far more dangerous for the other driver than for them. With a growl, he pulled off onto the shoulder and slammed on the brakes. The Winnie slid a few more feet across the fine dirt, and they jerked to a stop. "Lily. Hey." He caught her hand instinctively and rubbed it gently. "Oh, man. I thought you were—"

"They did it."

"What?"

"Romeo, they finally did it. Oh, my God."

He squeezed her hand but received nothing in

response. "I don't know what's going on, but you had some kind of seizure, I think, and you were bleeding, and there's a hospital in—"

"No. No, don't take me there. We can't... I can't..." Lily slid her fingers out of his and raised both hands to her mouth. "There's no way she survived that. I didn't know if I would. She's... I felt everything."

"Okay, slow down."

"She's gone. I know she's gone. I felt her, only for a second, and there was so much pain." Her breath caught in her throat and she found she couldn't breathe at all except in short, sharp bursts that hardly pulled in any air.

"Woah, woah." Romeo almost tore his seatbelt in half before he finally threw the buckle against the seat. Quickly, he climbed over the center console and sat beside her, running a hand through her hair. "Okay, breathe, Lily. That's all you need to think about right now. Just breathe." He took deep breaths with her for a minute until she could finally catch her breath and the panic subsided.

A cold shiver raced up her spine, and she tried to blink away the tears that came on way too quickly. "She's gone."

"We don't know that, Lil. There's no way to be sure about it."

Lily turned her head slowly to meet his gaze and almost couldn't see him. "Romeo, I felt it. I felt her, and what they did to her, and then nothing. I felt her leave."

"Maybe she only passed out like you did." He shook his head and caught her hand again. "Hey, listen to me. Whatever they did to her freaked us both out, okay? Because it affected you too." She leaned away from him, but he pulled her back. "Lily. Stop. We don't know for sure."

"Then why did I feel that?" She pulled in a deep breath and tried to exhale slowly, although it came out in another shudder. "It felt like she died. And I was right there with her." She sniffed, wiped under her nose with her forearm, and glanced at the flakes of dried blood. "This is mine?" She touched her upper lip again and felt more dry blood there too.

"Yeah. You..." He swallowed. "That was a bad one. Aside from the fact that I almost crashed the RV into another car, I am so glad you woke up."

She shook her head and squinted through the windshield. "Where are we?"

"We're about to reach Sirte, I think."

"How long was I out?"

"A little over an hour."

She looked at him again and finally squeezed his hand in return. "Are you okay?"

Romeo tilted his head and shrugged. "I'm better now."

"I'm so sorry."

"You don't have to be sorry." He leaned forward, kissed her temple, and wrapping his arms around her quickly when she pressed her forehead into his chest and took in another ragged breath. "You didn't do anything wrong, Lily. I'm only glad you're okay."

"For now." She realized she'd clutched a fistful of his shirt and gently released it. "I don't even know how okay I am. That was...that was definitely the worst thing I can think of right now. I just..." She took a moment to pull herself together, nodded, and leaned back in the seat. "Don't take me to a hospital. I'm fine. I need to look for her." She tried to stand, but he held her shoulders and eased her down.

"Maybe it's a good idea to wait. Only for a few minutes."

"She might not have a few minutes. I'm serious. I have to try this."

"Lily, you were convulsing on the floor and bleeding from your ears. I think you need to rest for a second. At least let me get you some water. See if there's anything else we need to address first with you before you...exhaust yourself again trying to pull out your raven totem. You haven't even learned exactly how to do that yet."

She stared at him, swallowed, and gritted her teeth. "I'm going to cast that spell, and I'm going to look for her. If she's still alive, I'll find her."

"Lily—"

"I really don't want to have to force you out of my way, so please. Don't make me."

He studied the cold glint in her eyes, one of which twitched a little as she stared obdurately at him. Knowing this was one standoff he'd never manage to win, Romeo nodded. "Okay." He stood from the center console, stepped over it, and extended a hand although he almost thought she'd refuse his help. She took it, though, and let him support her up and out of the passenger seat. "I want you to find her too," he added gently and released her hand. "But you don't have to try to use your raven totem. I don't think that's the safest thing for you right now."

Lily tilted her head and bit her lip as she regarded him with a trace of impatience in her expression. "I don't have any other choice."

"You do, actually."

"What?"

He scratched the back of his head, gritted his teeth, and ran a hand through his dark curls. "I can't believe I'm actually saying this, but at this point, it might even be safer than you using magic that takes far more out of you than you have right now." She opened her mouth to question him again, but he stopped her with a raised hand. "Just... hold on. I'll be right back." He turned halfway, paused, and decided against whatever he was going to say and went quickly into the bedroom.

Lily grimaced and focused on breathing slowly. *I'll find you, Mom. If you're still...if you're there, I'll find you. We're so close.* She scratched an itch below her ear and found another crust of dried blood beneath her fingernails. "Jeeze."

Romeo cleared his throat as he stepped out of the bedroom and moved through the RV toward her. "Okay. I didn't say anything about it because I'm fairly sure we both feel the same way. I also hoped we had enough on our own that you wouldn't need it." He stopped in front of her and stared at his clenched fist.

"Please, just tell me," she said, amazed that after everything, her voice didn't shake at all.

With a sigh, he settled his gaze on her. "This is probably our best bet."

"Romeo..."

He opened his hand and glanced at it again. She thought she was seeing things until she closed her eyes for a moment and opened them again with no change to what rested in his hand. "How did you get that?" She pointed vaguely at the silver heron coin that winked at her beneath the Winnebago's overhead lights.

"I picked it up before the fight in Ozias' bunker." He shifted his weight and stared over her shoulder at the dashboard. "I shoved it in my pocket before I shifted and decided I'd save it for an emergency. You know, like this one."

She bit her lip and eyed the heron coin. "And you weren't gonna say anything about it unless we really needed it. Like right now."

The werewolf shook his head. "I'm sorry. If you're angry, I totally get that and I can deal with it. You thought it was gone, and it was easier to play it off like that. I know you didn't mean for anything to happen like it did in Oitylo. Ozias and his people knew that too. But it was... I mean, you summoned this out of the Winnie and all the way underground, right into your lap, Lil. I assume it was super-easy for you, and I didn't want you to worry about that part—"

"Okay." Lily held his shoulder gently and gave it a little squeeze. "Okay."

Romeo's gaze darted from the coin in his hand to her arm reaching toward him and finally to her eyes. "Okay?"

"I'm not mad. I probably would've done the same thing if things were switched the other way around." She nodded. "I'm glad you picked it up and that you thought about what we might need down the road instead of ignoring everything else before that fight in the bunker. Honestly, I'm really glad you didn't tell me you had it until right now."

He blew out a breath of relief and gave her a sheepish smile. "I guess I was worried about a whole lotta nothin', huh?"

"Maybe." She slid her hand down his arm and stopped at his wrist, not quite ready yet to touch the heron coin once again. "Maybe not. Thank you."

"You're welcome." He nodded at the couch. "If you're gonna do this, we should probably sit, right?"

"Definitely." She went to the couch first, stopped, and turned to point at him. "Whatever happens, though, no hospitals, okay?"

"You were bleeding out of your ears, Lil—"

"No hospitals. If I'm caught up in a place like that with a new, giant target on my back again, the Black Heron's not gonna care how many innocent people they have to mow down to get to me. There are too many innocent people in a hospital."

His nostrils flared, but he finally sighed, nodded, and came to sit beside her. "Okay. No hospitals. If anything happens to you, do you think Bentley could talk a werewolf through how to bring you back?"

Lily smirked, knowing he was mostly joking but that there was still a trace of truth in there. He was scared. "Unless you tapped into the Black Heron's free-magic experiments, you won't have any luck with spells. But yeah, Bentley could definitely talk you through how to get some potions, at the very least."

"Does he know anyone in Libya?"

"I don't think so."

"Well, I guess we covered as much of a contingency as possible. Are you ready, then?"

She pulled her legs up onto the couch and crossed them beneath her, then stared at the silver heron coin resting in his open palm. "Yep. You know we gotta be on our toes when I'm done, right? I don't know how much time we'll have before they storm down the road."

"I'm ready for that, Lil. No problem."

"Good answer." With a deep breath, she pulled up the last memory of her mom's face—dirt-streaked, gaunt, but still determined—and stretched her hand out to touch the coin.

TWENTY-FIVE

The air sucking out of her lungs wasn't nearly as intense this time, only a little pinch. In the next moment, Lily registered the darkness of the Black Heron network, and it responded instantly to what she wanted. The red lines streaked from her location in every direction, but they were little more than a blur before the tunnel of images narrowed in front of her vision and showed her exactly where she needed to go.

The vision took her directly across the desert, heading southeast along the Mediterranean before cutting almost directly south. She soared over towns, over brown, dry land, and over paved roads and packed, sunbaked dirt roads. Finally, she saw the same nondescript patch of earth beside an empty road. The only reason she knew it was the same place was because the air across the road shimmered with the orange-brown light exactly like it had the last time she'd seen it. Other than that, there was nothing else there.

Wait... What's that?

A tiny flicker of yellow light rose from the barren, dusty earth. Lily wanted to move closer to see what could have been a bottlecap reflecting the sunlight or something that was actually important for her to see—to remember. She couldn't move, though, as the network's tunnel only took her so far and would only show her so much. As she strained to make out the source of the yellow flicker in the dirt, she didn't notice that the orange-brown shimmer in the air solidified, grew, and became a face that hovered in the air.

It was giant, the size of an actor's face projected on an IMAX screen. The man had a short, pointed goatee and one completely opaque eye and he stared directly at her.

The vision lurched forward, and she was shoved up against the shimmering wall of light that had become the man's face. It was all she could see, and if she'd been there in body, she would have leaned away from the sneer he brought to bear on her. "You are so resilient, little witch." The man's voice growled all around her and drove all other thoughts from her mind. "And foolish." His face receded into the shimmering orange light to reveal the man's entire figure. He wore an old-fashioned smoking jacket, the high collar turned down neatly along his shoulders. When he stepped back and stretched an arm behind him, she saw a huge study, full bookshelves lining both walls, and a fire crackling in the hearth on the left. There was so much to take in—too much—but it had to be a reliquary with all the glass-doored cabinets filled with jars, glowing metal tools, and an orb that spun continually in midair.

In the center of it all, kneeling in front of the low coffee table between two massive, wing-backed armchairs, was Greta Antony.

"Come and join your mother, Lily. Complete our circle. She is waiting for you, and now, so are we. Most of us, at any rate." The man chuckled, lunged forward and shoved both hands out toward her with a snarl.

She was thrown back across the bare earth, over the dirt road, and back through the tunnel. All the images she'd been shown blurred past her at even greater speeds and the red lines of the network crossed over each other again and again and glowed brighter until the only thing she could see was one massive flash of red.

The next thing she knew, she was sprawled on her back on top of the kitchen table in the Winnie, her head throbbing and her legs caught at an awkward angle over the back of the booth.

"Lily?" Romeo was at her side in an instant, the silver heron coin forgotten on the couch. He eased an arm beneath her upper back and helped her to sit on the table. Carefully, he turned her toward him and held her face in both hands while he examined her for more blood or signs of another seizure or anything that might mean she wasn't actually okay. "Hey, you gotta say something. Please."

Lily closed her eyes and shook her head quickly and when she opened them again, her blurry vision finally focused. She brought her hands up to his wrists and gave them a reassuring squeeze. "She's alive." When she looked at him, his eyes were glistening.

"Sure, that's something." He puffed out another deep breath. "Does everything feel okay?"

"She's okay. I mean, they have her, but she's okay."

"I meant with you." He leaned closer until his face was directly in front of hers and studied her gaze. "Are you okay?"

"Yeah. I'm fine." It was hard to nod like she wanted to with his hands on either side of her face. "All I got was south. Southeast, kind of."

He merely nodded but didn't release his hold on her yet. "Was there anything different? Anything we can work with?"

"Only a dirt road in the middle of nowhere and some kind of spell in the air—almost like a ward. Like how the Romani hid their village, remember? But someone talked to me through it. A man with a fake eye, I think."

"Huh." He lowered his hands slowly from her face and settled them on her shoulders for a moment before he finally let her go. "Did you actually see your mom?"

"He showed her to me. I don't know exactly where. She was in this library, or a reliquary..." Her head pounded again, which made it hard to concentrate on what she wanted to tell him. "There was something else there. In the ground. It was like a—" She narrowed her eyes and turned slowly where she sat on the table to look over her shoulder. There was the bright chord of glowing yellow light, exactly like it always was. "Oh, my God. The light."

"Okay, if you have a sensitivity to light now, Lil, that's not a good sign."

"No, not that. I mean—" She pointed in the direction of the yellow beam. "What direction is that?"

"Um..." He chuckled. "I never actually thought I'd

wish I had a compass. Hold on." He hurried to the front of the Winnie, retrieved his phone, and pulled up the GPS. The tip of the little blue triangle that showed him where they were moved as he spun toward Lily. He stood in front of the table again and moved his phone until it was lined up with her pointing finger. "Southwest, basically. A little more south, maybe."

"Oh, jeez." Lily ran her hands through her hair, slid off the table, and turned. The yellow beam streamed directly ahead of her now, directly from her chest to disappear through the side of the Winnie. She knew it would keep going once she stepped outside. That it would always point in that direction. "That's what this is. This whole time, I thought it was...well, I didn't have any idea." She looked up at Romeo with wide eyes and chose to ignore his gaping mouth and the fact that he was still completely clueless. "I saw something in the network. Only the smallest trace of yellow light on the ground. I didn't get a chance to see what it was before the man started talking to me, and then he literally tossed me out again—"

"Lily?"

"Yeah."

"Pretend I don't know anything at all. I can't follow your train of thought right now."

"Right." She nodded. "We simply have to follow the light. This thing"—she pointed at the beam he couldn't see —"that's kept me awake and never goes away. I can see it but you can't but I'm almost positive it's leading me precisely to that stretch of open road in the middle of nowhere. Right to her. That's what we have to follow. That point of light in the dirt is like a...like a pinned location. I don't know how, but that's how we find her."

Romeo nodded slowly and put everything together in his own way. "What are the chances that pinned location is simply one more clue your mom left for you to find?"

"I'd say they're reasonably high. I didn't think she could do it because they still have her but obviously, she did." She stared at the yellow beam where it vanished through the wall and uttered a surprised laugh. "She's still leaving me clues."

"And she's still alive."

She whirled to look at him and remembered the rest of it. The frown settled on her brow felt tight and made her head pound even more. "The man who spoke to me...he basically gave me an open invitation to come to get her."

"That doesn't sound like a trap in any way whatsoever." He scowled and scratched the back of his head.

"But all the Black Heron members who targeted us have wanted me for something, right? It's obviously not to kill me anymore." She rubbed the back of her aching head and found the tender place where she'd thumped it against the table. "He literally threw me out of the network and across the Winnie," she muttered.

"It was intense."

She looked at him and gave him a small smile. "I'll be fine. He said they were waiting for me—my mom and the Black Heron Society. But not all of them."

He frowned. "Like the Frankenstein magicals who wanted to take you in for experiments. Is that what you're thinking?"

"Yeah. The ones who haven't managed to blow themselves up yet are looking for me too. Maybe it started with all of them wanting to bring me in and hand me over. I don't know. But it would be almost impossible for anyone to control that many magicals all over the world. Not completely."

"So the Black Heron Society has split into factions." Romeo folded his arms and stared at the floor. "The ones who have your mom and want you to show up to complete whatever this stupid circle is. And then the ones who already had a taste of that messed-up stolen magic on a much smaller scale. They want you because the higherups want you, but not to bring you to your mom."

Lily huffed out a sigh and threw her arms up. "This is getting ridiculous."

"It's always been ridiculous. Remember that werewolf in Canada? The one who chased us out of that club for magicals?"

"The one who cast spells like a witch before he suckerpunched you?"

Romeo frowned quickly and released a surprised laugh. "It wasn't a sucker punch."

"Well you didn't go down, so it doesn't really matter."

"It does matter, but—" He closed his eyes and chuckled again. "Not as much as this. That werewolf had someone else's magic, Lily, because of the Black Heron's experiments leading up to this giant, magical free-for-all spell they're trying to whip up. So yeah. If they gave the wrong kind of people access to even a little taste of magic that didn't belong to them—"

"They're all the wrong kind of people." A wave of dizziness rushed over her, and she braced herself for a few seconds against the table.

"Are you okay?"

"I'm only a little dizzy."

"Gotcha." He turned quickly to get her a bottle of water from the fridge and snapped the cap open on his way back before he handed it over.

"Thanks." She drank as much as she could and managed to find her feet again. "If we're right, things actually got weirdly more complicated."

"Yeah, I didn't think that was possible until now."

She lowered her head and decided to drink a little more water, just in case. "The head of the Black Heron hierarchy...they're the ones who want me to keep going. To find my mom and deliver myself up to their giant dark spell, I guess."

"And the crazy underlings want to steal you first, experiment with your magic, and then take you in and collect their prize."

Lily snorted. "No one's getting a prize for that. But we're gonna go get my mom. And after that, we'll do whatever we have to do to make sure their circle, whatever it is, doesn't get anywhere near completed."

"Man, I really wish I knew what the heck that stupid thing's supposed to be. Or do."

She smiled and gave his chest a gentle pat, feeling like herself again despite a night without sleep and having been thrown across her own RV. "Careful what you wish for, buddy."

TWENTY-SIX

"Can you map us a good route to get us...I guess simply southwest through the country, right?" Lily screwed the lid back onto the bottle of water and headed toward the front of the Winnie again.

"Definitely." Romeo joined her and slid into the driver's seat, already working it up on his phone. "You have no idea how far southwest, huh?"

"Nope. But when this super-annoying beam of light stops pointing at anything, I guess we'll know we're there."

"Got it." He placed his phone into the cupholder and started the engine. "Uh-oh."

"Okay, new rule. Any uh-ohs are followed up by a number on a scale of one to ten."

He looked at her and pointed at the gas gauge behind the steering wheel. "On the 'this is bad' scale, it's a two. I'd give an almost empty tank a nine-point-five on the priority scale, though."

She sighed and rubbed her cheeks. "We won't get very far without gas."

"Not unless you have a flying carpet stashed away in here somewhere." He smirked and shifted into drive.

"Those are much harder to come by than you think."

"Wait, flying carpets are real?"

"Romeo, we were ferried across the Mediterranean in half an hour, the last moments of which we spent riding on the top of this RV, and you actually watched me catapult onto the table because I touched a coin." She pressed her lips together and studied his profile as they moved onto the road and headed toward Sirte, the town now faintly visible a few miles ahead of them. "How are you still surprised by things like flying carpets?"

"I only..." He laughed and ran a hand through his hair. "The only magic I'd really seen before you showed up at my house in the middle of the summer came from you and your mom. Not much of it applies to werewolves. I dunno. Maybe I wouldn't question it at all if we actually were riding a flying carpet."

"Fair enough." She leaned against the passenger seat and watched the city grow larger and closer ahead of them. "To be clear, though, I'm fairly sure genies aren't a real thing."

"No genies. No magic lamps. Got it."

"No...no there are still magic lamps."

He thumped his hand against the steering wheel. "Now you tell me." With a broad grin, he shook his head and cast her a few quick glances before he returned his full attention to the road. "How come genies aren't a real thing? The rest of the magical world couldn't find a place for them, or what?"

"Seriously?" Lily burst into laughter and winced at the throbbing pain it brought to the back of her head again. "Try not to make me laugh so hard for a while."

"But I'm really good at it." He smirked and lifted one shoulder in a half-hearted shrug.

"Where did you think all the stories about magic came from in the first place? Like the kids' movies and books and everything."

"I..." Romeo startled and couldn't come up with the witty response he wanted. "Okay, that's a good point. Hey, did you know all this when we were kids?"

"Of course."

"So you watched all those movies with me and didn't even think to tell me that parts of them were real?"

She snorted. "My mom told me not to."

"What? You and Greta conspired to keep me in the dark about all the magical things you already knew."

"Well, now you know."

"Oh, yeah." He laughed. "Now I know that half my childhood was a lie." He turned to raise his eyebrows at her and tried to look completely shocked.

"That's not tr—Romeo!" Lily pointed out the windshield, and with a hiss of surprise, He jerked the Winnie's steering wheel in time to avoid hitting the half-dozen magicals who'd materialized in thin air directly in front of them. The tires squealed across the highway, and he corrected the swerve, his hands moving deftly over each other as he attempted to regain control of the wheel.

One of the magicals lunged toward them anyway, thumped against the hood, and rolled up onto the windshield with a flash of green light before tumbling back onto the highway. "What the hell?" He glanced in the side mirror.

"Was he trying to get hit?" Lily shouted. "Do you see—"

They lurched forward when a quick succession of magical blasts struck the rear of the RV and bright-red streaks of energy crackled along the vehicle's exterior. Lily jerked away from the passenger-side window when they streaked across the glass. "Ow!" He lifted both hands from the steering wheel when the red sparks sent an electric jolt through his fingers. "I am really tired of being attacked in this thing." His hands clamped on the steering wheel one more and he accelerated in an effort to gain distance between themselves and the ambushers.

"I can't believe I forgot." She clutched the silver-framed mirror charm clasped around her neck—her mom's first clue and the one thing they knew would turn the Black Heron's tracker on her off after she'd used the coin. They'd already tested it once. *Unravel the most powerful setback.* She closed her eyes and focused on the mirror's single purpose. It gave off a little hum beneath her fingers, and she shook her head. "That should've made us dark again."

"Yeah, but these guys already know they found us. We're heading for the city, Lil."

"Don't go there. Take this exit instead." She pointed at the next sign a little ahead.

"Good call." Romeo glanced at the on-ramp on their right, where three beat-up sedans raced way faster than normal people trying to get onto any highway. "What are these lunatics doing?" He pressed on the gas pedal before he recalled that his boot was already holding it against the floor. "Woah. Woah."

The cars rocketed onto the highway in front of them and turned. Tires squealed over the asphalt and they drifted ahead of the Winnie. When they stopped, two balls of green fire hurtled through one of the open windows toward the young couple.

With a roar of frustration, he jerked on the wheel and swung them into the other lane of traffic, which was mostly clear except for a large van barreling toward them out of the city. The van's driver didn't so much as blare on the horn or even apply the brakes.

"Watch out—watch out!" Lily braced herself on the armrests and couldn't help but push both feet down against the floor in front of her.

"I'm trying." The Winnie rocked on its left side when Romeo jerked the wheel even harder to the left again to avoid the van. The right tires bounced back onto the highway with a jolt and a short squeal, and in the next moment, they hurtled in the opposite direction.

"The van is right behind us." She stared at the side mirror. "It's coming up fast."

"Yeah, and there's a group of crazy idiots standing in the middle of the highway up here." He jerked a hand toward the windshield. "The other guys came in cars. So Sirte's full of Black Heron members, or what?"

"Hey, focus on getting us out of this first, okay? We can speculate later."

"I can make it past 'em." Romeo nodded and hoped the Winnie could at least get up past eighty before he tried to bulldoze through the line of magicals on the road.

"Not through that, you can't." She stared with wide eyes at the warded wall being cast across the highway.

Five of the society members had joined their magic together to erect it. A sludgy black film rose from their outstretched hands and glistened like wet tar as it rose higher and higher in front of them. The sixth member in the line flung a salvo of silver streaking lights toward them that pelted the hood and the bottom of the windshield. One of the projectiles stuck in the glass and Lily stared at the dangerously sharp tip of what looked like a tiny dagger poking through the spiderwebbed crack. A thin, purple line of smoke trailed from the tip.

"What's that?" Romeo shouted.

She clenched her fist and flicked a hand at the tiny magical dagger. A burst of compulsion energy flung it out of the windshield and left a fist-sized hole in the glass. "It's gone." She coughed when the stench of steamed broccoli left out for a week stung her nose. "Man, that's nasty."

"Lily, I can't keep making hairpin turns on the highway."

"So let's do some off-roading." She jabbed her thumb toward her window where the blazing yellow beam attached to her streamed across the brown, open land.

"Yep." He swung the wheel to the right and the Winnie bumped off the shoulder and into the fine sand

and dirt. Something else pelted the back of the RV behind them, but there weren't any more sparks.

Lily clenched her teeth once again so she wouldn't bite her tongue off as they trundled over the open ground and kicked up a spray of dust and pebbles behind them. Romeo's growl shook in his throat over the uneven terrain and his hold tightened on the steering wheel. "They're seriously desperate." She leaned forward to get a better view in the side mirror. "The cars and the van are following us. I have no idea about the other guys."

"Do you think they have less gas in their tanks than we do?"

She looked at him and caught his worried frown. "Probably not."

"Great."

Her hand thumped the automatic window button and she rolled her window all the way down. "Keep driving as straight as you can and try not to go over any really large rocks. Or bushes." She unbuckled her seatbelt.

"What are you doing?"

"Fighting back. Just keep going as long as you can."

He growled again and shook his head but didn't say anything else.

TWENTY-SEVEN

Lily shoved her feet between the side of the Winnie and the passenger seat and hooked them in the tightest position she could find. She sat on the window frame, steadied herself, and leaned back a little through the window.

A blaze of purple light erupted toward her from the open passenger-side window of the van that raced across the sands in pursuit. She ducked and had enough time to throw up a warded shield that deflected the second attack. The van swerved out to the right, presumably so the driver and the passenger could both acquire a better target on the witch who leaned halfway out of the RV. She tried to focus on her black cloud spell, but the society members threw one attack after the other. Instead, she raised another warded shield and fired two columns of blue flames at the van's passenger. One of them caught on the man's sleeve and immediately erupted on his shirt. His screams echoed over the crunch of tires on gravel and the roar of the

Winnebago's rumbling engine. The van's driver paid his cohort no attention but increased speed to try to flank the RV.

Lily slid off the window frame and crawled into the passenger seat, her feet under her as she sat on her heels and prepared herself to try again. "I can't get enough of a window. They won't—"

Green light blazed beside them before a massive ball of energy, air, and wind pounded into the left side of the Winnie. Romeo shouted and wrenched the steering wheel. The RV rocked on its wheels again, and she was amazed by how slowly she seemed to fly through the open window. She put both her hands out —not to catch herself but to cast the same physical compulsion spell she'd tried the first time Watcher had launched them from the sea and up onto the cliffs. The force of that spell blasting from both her palms slowed her descent enough that she no longer hurtled forward but floated rather gently. Her feet touched the dry earth, and her shoes skidded a little before she really found her footing and righted herself.

At that moment, the instinct she didn't know she had took over.

The van raced toward her across the desert, and she pelted its front left tire with a massive stream of her crackling red sparks from both hands. Metal screeched, and she caught a glimpse of the van's passenger still batting at the blue flames that consumed his shirt before the van lifted onto its back wheels, rolled away from her, and rolled end over end in almost slow motion.

The car that had come alongside the RV on the left

clipped the front of the Winnebago as its driver tried to drive in front of Romeo and turn to reach her. The Winnie rocked toward her, and she cast another compulsion spell along its entire length to right it again. The vehicle lurched to a stop with a spray of pebbles, and she turned to face the other two cars who'd come to their own scrambled stop in the sand beside Romeo. Two of them were between her and the RV, and the one that had clipped the Winnebago could be seen peering out from behind her front bumper.

Shards of something that whistled alarmingly in flight burst from the passenger window of the closest car, and she deflected it quickly with another warded shield. Doors opened, magicals exited, and Lily Antony clapped sharply.

It took her no time at all to bring up the roiling mass of her black cloud spell between her palms. She pulled her arms apart, farther and farther, and the closest magical—a witch with wildly spikey, green-dyed hair and a thick tan vest—raised both hands and snarled. Purple, snaking vines launched from his palms and whipped and writhed through the air toward her.

A tendril of her own black cloud darted out from the source between her hands and severed the lashing vines in one snap. The witch who'd cast them screamed and clutched his bleeding hand to his chest. Lily pulled her arms farther apart and allowed the black cloud to build. Lights flashed at her from the other side as the Black Heron members pelted her with one attack after the other. She couldn't see what her own spell did to theirs anymore, but she could feel it.

A snarl rose from the Winnie, and a massive form of

shaggy black fur darted through the open window. Romeo launched himself at the closest society member—a warlock, she thought vaguely—before the air in front of her erupted with snarls and screams of agony and shouts of rage.

When her arms reached their full extension, the black cloud loomed like a dark curtain in front of her. Her chest felt like it was about to explode until she simply let it all go and another shadow-bird hurtled from her chest with a resounding boom, whipped up the dust and dirt around her, and took the roiling, flashing mass of her spell with it.

The huge raven totem she'd released spanned as wide as the RV was long. Its wings of smoke and ash and Optatus power cut a path toward the magicals who had divided their attention between Romeo and Lily. It plowed through all five of them and cut them down where they stood without a sound rising from any of their throats. Finally, the huge black raven screeched and rocketed skyward at tremendous speed.

Romeo crouched on all fours and snarled at the bodies scattered over the desert. None of them moved.

"Woah." Lily gasped for breath, her head pounding again with another rush of dizziness. "I think...is that it?"

He licked what looked like blood off his muzzle and fixed her with his silver eyes. A low whine escaped him. When she staggered in the dirt, he trotted toward her but cast a few glances back toward the society members she'd annihilated with a single spell.

"That was a lot." She put a hand to her throbbing forehead and blinked. "Are you okay?"

The werewolf approached her again and she held out

her hand, anticipating the feel of his thick, shaggy black fur beneath her fingertips. Seconds before he reached her, a shimmering wall of electric blue flared up between them. The tip of his black nose struck the wall and the barrier snapped with angry energy. He leapt back and snarled again.

"What a show!" The witch behind them clapped her red-gloved hands and laughed. Lily whirled and scowled at the six society members who'd teleported in front of them on the highway. The woman with the gloves smoothed a hand over her blonde hair, which was already tied back into a severely neat bun with not a single strand out of place. Her sunglasses flashed in the light as she stepped toward them.

The Optatus witch summoned a handful of red sparks and held them out beside her, ready to attack when needed. "So which kind are you, then, huh?"

Romeo prowled along the shimmering blue wall between them, testing its limits and getting shocked again every few feet.

The woman turned slowly to eye the other magicals who walked up behind her. The huge, hulking man on the far left glowed with intermittent flashes of green and purple, and he limped from throwing himself at the RV and being tossed onto the road again. "That's a very strange question to ask." The woman stopped, tilted her head, and smiled. "Were you hoping for someone else?"

"I have no idea who you are." Lily raised her other hand, where more sparks flared to life, and the magicals behind the woman with red gloves all readied some form of their own spells in raised hands. "But I can't tell if you're one of the idiots who want me for experiments or if you're gonna take me exactly where I want to be."

"Aw." The woman pursed her lips in mock dejection and shrugged. "We're a mixed bag." She moved slowly and almost insolently to remove her sunglasses and reveal two glowing eyes—one the bright, flashing silver of a werewolf before a shift, the other the deep, crimson-red of a warlock who'd given up a part of herself to work exclusively with blood magic. "I will say, though, that I'm very interested in what you just did." The woman nodded toward the bodies sprawled behind Romeo, whose hackles stood stiffly as he bared his fangs and paced on the other side of the blue wall.

"You won't get anything from me," Lily said. The red sparks on her fingertips grew larger and hissed and crackled in both hands.

The hybrid Black Heron member laughed, and a few chuckles rose from those who followed her. The woman standing to the leader's right tossed her hair out of her face, and what looked like an actual third eye stared from the middle of her forehead. "I don't have to take anything from you now, little witch." The woman with the red gloves grinned and spread her arms. "I only have to take you with me."

"That is not gonna happen." Lily tossed her red sparks at the woman, but a second wall of shimmering blue magic flared to life a few feet in front of her. Her attack spell snapped against the ward or shield or whatever it was and spilled red streaks to either side before they fizzled out completely. The young witch scowled and stared at the laughing society members. "Let me out and fight me."

"Not yet." The woman snapped her fingers, and the blue walls both in front of and behind Lily flashed.

She frowned darkly when she realized she was enclosed in an actual box of warded magic, all the sides of which now closed in around her. "A box." Lily looked at the witch-werewolf-warlock's mismatched eyes and wrinkled her nose. "Really?"

The woman merely shrugged. "It seems to be working so far." She snapped her gloved fingers, and the magicals behind her spread out around the enclosure. The beefy guy with a limp leaned toward the shrinking blue box and leered at her. Romeo launched himself at the green-and-purple-flashing magical and flung him to the ground. The man howled and released a spray of blue sparks as he tried to fight the werewolf off.

"And get that thing under control, huh?" The leader nodded at the woman with the third eye, who chuckled and pushed her sleeves up her arms.

Lily clapped briskly and summoned her Optatus spell again. She rushed it a little because the third eye on the witch who stepped toward Romeo now pulsed with a sickly yellow-green glow.

"You can't do anything from in there," the hybrid taunted. "I've seen many people try."

The young witch's arms shook as she pulled them apart, which became increasingly more difficult as the sides of the magical blue box closed in even more. Her elbow bumped against one wall and a jolt of electricity seared through her arm, but she kept her focus on the spell and the feeling of sending her raven totem out. She glared at the hybrid leader. "But you didn't get all of me."

A momentary flicker of fear and realization creased the woman's brow. A screech sounded from directly above them, and she looked up.

Lily's raven totem swooped down from the sky, its wingtips streaming black smoke behind it as the rest of her Optatus magic grew within its churning, flashing black body. The massive bird dove and impacted with the society members to scatter them in all directions. A blaze of fierce, heightened energy coursed through her. She threw her hands out to her sides and screamed at the endless jolts of pain that streaked up her arms and into her chest when her hands broke through the warded blue box. The spells folded in on themselves, the box dissipated to nothing, and everything around her became a vortex of howling black smoke and screaming society members and the telltale snarl of Romeo leaping from one of them to the next.

The power of it tossed Lily's hair around her face and whipped up funnels of dirt and a few dried plants from the ground. A red glove stretched toward her through the blackness, but the black cloud yanked the hand away before it could release the flames that flickered at the hybrid's fingertips.

In only a few seconds, everything fell still. The black cloud slowly faded to a few stray wisps of smoke that curled lazily upward. She stood in silence and stared at the bodies strewn across the baked earth. The young witch swayed a little and the corners of her vision darkened. Warm hands caught her shoulders from behind, and she leaned back against Romeo's bare skin.

"Okay, easy." He gave her shoulders a gentle squeeze and brought his lips to her ear to whisper, "We're all good."

She glanced at her shaking hands. The bandages on her wrists had been shredded when she'd broken through the warded box that had held her captive. A few streaks of blue lines flared up her forearms beneath the tattered bandages, then disappeared. "I have no idea what I just did."

"I think the only thing that matters right now is that you did it. And we can get going, yeah?"

Lily stared at the dozen bodies strewn around her, the cars, and the rolled van a little beyond the carnage. "I did all this."

"You did what you had to do, Lil. That's it. Come on. We need to keep going."

"Are they..."

He sighed. "I don't know. We have to go. Half of them came from the city. There might not be a tracker on you anymore, but there are probably more of these people and they're bound to know something's wrong." He glanced over his shoulder at the highway far behind them and the tops of a few cars glinting in the sun as they passed. "Not to mention whatever authorities are gonna respond to a number of cars that took a detour off the highway. Come on." He pulled her gently by the shoulders toward the Winnie.

A groan rose from the rolled van, and the driver,

although hanging upside-down by his seatbelt, raised a hand and conjured a ball of purple flickering light. "You—"

Lily turned toward him and pointed. A burst of black smoke streaked from her fingertip and struck the frame of the van to spin it sideways in the dirt. The driver's spell launched out over the desert sand and disappeared.

Romeo cleared his throat and guided her back toward the RV. "Okay, you're throwing tiny pieces of your black-cloud spell now, and I'm totally naked. We need to regroup."

They reached the Winnie's side door, which was dented and buckled a little where she had hit it with her compulsion spell to prevent it from rolling like the van. With a grunt, Romeo fiddled with the handle and finally jerked the door open.

"I can fix that," she muttered.

"Yep. Later. Right now, we're leaving." He helped her up the steps into the RV and kept a hand on her back as she walked slowly to the front. "All right. Sit and rest. I got it from here."

She felt like she almost melted into the passenger seat, barely aware of her own hands as they caught the seatbelt to strap herself in. Romeo tugged his jeans on, zipped them, and didn't bother with a shirt.

"Can you still see that yellow light?" He slumped into the driver's seat, buckled up, and shoved the gearshift into drive. Lily had only enough energy to point slightly to their right, her finger following the blazing line of the light leading her directly to her mom's last clue. "Got it. You know what? You're getting much better at navigating."

With a smile, he stretched all the way over the center console, patted her thigh, looked at her, and realized she wasn't in a place for jokes or probably any talking at all right now. Rather than even attempt it, he simply gave her leg a little squeeze and steered them back on course as much as he could guess.

Lily's arm dropped into her lap, and despite the fact that the brilliant light of the beam showing her the way still flared behind her eyelids, she finally drifted off to sleep.

Lily was convinced she smelled smoke. She almost ignored it and wanted nothing more than to slide back into sleep again. Romeo's mumbled curse and heaving sigh told her something was wrong. Her eyes opened and she squinted against the blaze of the yellow beam before she turned her head toward him. "What's wrong?"

"I thought we had enough gas." He removed his hands from the steering wheel and turned to look at her as the Winnie rolled to a stop in the middle of open ground. "We're like...I don't know. Ten miles from the road I tried to get us to."

"Oh." She looked out over the dunes stretching into the distance and wrinkled her nose. "Ten miles isn't that far."

"To walk? Maybe not. But we can't simply leave the Winnie here. And I'm not leaving you alone."

She smirked. "Who said I'd be the one to stay here?"

He lowered his head warningly and looked at her from beneath a stern brown. "No."

"So leave her in nuetral and we'll push."

"You wanna push an RV ten miles across the desert? Which I'm fairly sure is the Sahara Desert. Or at least it's about to be."

Lily folded her arms and smiled, although it felt tight and tired and not quite as playful as she wanted. "You have super-werewolf strength. I'll be a little gentler with the physical compulsion spells. We can take turns."

He stared at her in disbelief for a few moments, then snorted and shook his head. "How do you always make crazy ideas sound completely normal?"

"I think crazy situations might be our new normal." She leaned back in the passenger seat. "So they call for crazy ideas. Which actually makes them good ideas, by the way."

"It's weird that it actually makes sense, Lil."

"You should also be used to weird by now." Closing her eyes, she took a deep breath and tried not to think about whatever might be happening only a few miles off the highway with the crashed cars and the Black Heron society members they'd literally left in the dust.

"Are you okay?"

"Huh?" Her eyes flew open again, and she found way more concern on Romeo's face than she'd expected. "I'm fine. Really. I'm still tired and a little...shaken, maybe. Or it might be some kinda weird side effect of literally breaking through a ward with my arms." She glanced at the frayed bandages that hung from her wrists and started to peel them off. "These are basically useless now."

"All right. Why don't you get behind the wheel, and I'll start pushing."

"Sure."

She left a pile of tattered Ace bandages on the passenger seat when she climbed over the center console and took the wheel. Romeo looked at her from outside the driver-side door and he took her ankle gently to give it a little squeeze. "Let me know if you need anything, okay?"

"I will."

"I mean it. Even if you only feeling dizzy or something hurts. Or if anything else shows up that you weren't expecting."

"The Black Heron knows we're coming." She leaned toward him and patted his hand around her ankle. "I don't know if they're gonna try anything else with my mom again so soon. Not now that they know how close we are— which is hopefully very close. But I promise, if I feel anything else, I'll tell you. That doesn't mean I get to slip out of Winnie-pushing duty, though. You don't get to claim all the credit for getting us back on a road somewhere."

For a few seconds, he looked like he'd completely zoned out and hadn't heard a word she'd said. Then he slid his hand off her ankle, chuckled, and shook his head. "Literally nothing stops you, huh?"

She shrugged quickly and smirked. "Okay, I get slowed down sometimes, yeah. But stop me? Not so far."

"Okay." Romeo ran a hand through his curls and

stepped back. "I'll keep going until you tell me something's up or I get tired enough to change places."

Lily gave him a thumbs-up, and he closed the door, laughing. She waited for him to make his way behind the Winnebago to start pushing and watched him in the side mirror. He still only wore his jeans and boots, and she suddenly wished she had a way to watch him push the RV shirtless across Libya. The thought made her snort.

"Yeah, and then I wouldn't pay attention to anything else. Right now, Lily, follow the light. The bright, never-ending, super-annoying light stretching on forever." She scowled at the beam that continued to blaze from her torso and cutting a straight line through who knew what else lay ahead of them.

Slowly, the RV rolled forward and only picked up a little speed.

THE YOUNG WITCH did not intend to mess with their momentum by calling out to see if Romeo wanted to change places after forty minutes. "I think I underestimated him. He's gotta be getting tired." Lily glanced in the side mirror for the millionth time in those forty minutes but of course, didn't see anything but the side of the RV and the endless expanse of rolling sand in every direction. "And I can't remember the last time I've been this bored." She drummed her fingers on the steering wheel and finally dropped her hands into her lap. There wasn't anything new to look at, no scenery, and not even someone to talk to about how dull this trip had suddenly become. She glanced at the cup holder in the center console, but it was empty. "Where—" A hasty search revealed that Romeo's phone had fallen at some point between the center console and the driver's seat. She saw the corner of it glinting at her from where it had slid.

With a sigh, she felt for the lever beneath the seat to move it back so she could get his phone. Habit made her look up again quickly as if they were driving down a road and she was trying to multitask and not crash them into anything. "What am I doing? We're going like three miles an hour." The laugh died on her lips when she saw a thin, white shape ahead of them. It could have a mile away or maybe five times that given how hard it was to judge distance with nothing else around them. But it didn't disappear when she closed her eyes momentarily and opened them again.

"That's definitely a change." She pressed lightly on the Winnie's horn a few times and the RV crawled to a stop.

When she opened the door, Romeo was already jogging up toward her from the back. Sweat glistened on his face, neck, and shoulders. He wiped his forehead with his arm and looked at her with wide eyes.

"Before you ask, yes, I'm totally fine." Lily clambered out of the driver's seat and stepped away a few feet from the Winnie. "But I figured you'd wanna know about this." She gestured for him to come closer, and he complied reluctantly as he cast a quick glance behind them on the very small chance that there was actually anyone or anything else out there. When he turned toward her, she pointed across the flat ground ahead of the vehicle and a little off to the right. "You see that, right?"

He squinted and leaned forward before his eyes widened. "That could be a building. All the way out here in the middle of nowhere."

"Okay, good. I really hoped that I haven't started to see even more things no one else can." She sighed, nodded, and stared at the white square in the distance. "Admittedly, it's a little weird to see that. We're still far out from the closest road or highway, right?"

"Yep." He stuck his hands on his hips, wiped the sweat off his brow again, and regarded her with a questioning look. "What do you wanna do?"

"Well, I bet anyone who has a house or a business or something all the way out here needs a way to get out here. Maybe they have extra gas."

He frowned at her and the corners of his mouth twitched into not quite a smile. "That's stretching it a little far, don't you think?"

"Not any farther than you pushing an RV by yourself for the last forty minutes. Which you wouldn't have to do if whoever that is has gas and is willing to share. Or sell it. It doesn't matter. At this point, I'd pay someone to fill a few gas cans and bring them back so we can get going again." She grasped his shoulder and her hand almost slipped off. "You were really working at it, huh?" Laughing, she wiped her now sweaty hand on the leg of her pants.

"Yep." He grinned at her. "I saw that."

"What?"

"You were staring at me all covered in sweat. It's okay.

I'd be staring at me too." He ran a hand through his wet curls, made a face, and wiped his own hand on his jeans. "Yeah, let's go see what we can find, then."

"Do you want me to push this time?" Lily lifted her hands and wiggled her fingers. "I had more than enough time to rest up."

He glanced skeptically at her and rolled his eyes. "Yeah. Lemme get some water first and dry off before I sit and steer us toward a weird building in the middle of nowhere so we can maybe get some help."

She turned with him toward the Winnie. "There's that can-do attitude."

"Hey, I haven't lost the can-do attitude. I can do all kinds of things. Like this." He moved too quickly for her to anticipate and slung his arm around her shoulders, hugged her close, and laughing.

She only squirmed for a few seconds before she gave up any attempt to break free. "Mm."

"See? It's not that bad."

Her hand slid across his chest when she pushed him away, and he released her with a chuckle. "It feels the same," she said and wrinkled her nose, "but if you're gonna be all wet and slippery, it should be in the shower."

"Oh, yeah? It's a good thing we had that fixed."

"Yeah, 'cause you're gonna need it." They walked around the Winnie toward the side door, which was still buckled a little from essentially being punched by her magic. She paused, stretched toward the dented area around the handle and the side of the door, and spread her fingers. A violet light streamed from her fingers to the handle, and her simple repair charm twisted it back into place. The divots in the door popped out to their normal position, and she opened the side door with a little bow. "After you."

Romeo chuckled but waited for her to look at him first. "I'm glad you're feeling better."

"Me too. And I'll feel much better once we're not running on empty anymore and can get where we need to be. All this time, we managed to stay on top of gas and food and all the regular stuff people need to manage for a road trip."

With a smirk, he stepped into the vehicle. "It's not a regular road trip. We're doing very well if this is our only hiccup." Before she could correct him, he raised a finger and looked at her over his shoulder. "Our only logistical hiccup. I know there's a difference." She merely grinned and nodded. "Are you sure there isn't some kinda spell to, you know...magically pull gas out of nowhere? Like an emergency fuel charm or something?" He retrieved a bottle of water from the fridge and downed half of it in only a few swallows.

Lily shrugged carelessly and waited for the huge sigh she knew was coming. "No. No emergency fuel charms. Sorry."

He grimaced and headed back toward her. "It's a valid question."

"Sure. We wouldn't have had to stop for gas, food, or any other supplies if I could simply whip up whatever we needed out of thin air. I wish it worked that way."

"It worked in Ozias' bunker, didn't it? When you got

that coin out of the Winnie without ever coming up from underground?" Romeo stepped into the bathroom, found a towel, and quickly wiped himself dry.

"That wasn't conjuring something out of nothing, though." Lily swiped her hair back away from her face and frowned. "I'm sure that if I did that with gas or food, it'd essentially be theft by Optatus magic."

"Huh." He returned the towel and moved to the front, nodding as he considered it. "Yeah, that makes sense."

"And using that magic to steal, even if it's only gas for the Winnie..." Lily glanced at the cabinet above the kitchen sink where they'd stored the Varelos. "That feels like something leading down that slippery slope into going dark."

"Like the other Optatus witches Ozias talked about."

"Yeah." She squinted at the cabinet and put a few more pieces together through this strangely banal conversation despite what they'd been through today and how close they were to reaching the end of this insane trip. "I think I know what the Varelos was trying to tell me about my choice."

"What choice?"

"It said there were two ways for me to see. Through the dark or the light." She turned away from the kitchen and fixed him with a considering look. "I thought it was talking about what kind of witch I want to be. You know, a witch who still has a conscience or one who's willing to sell off pieces of herself to master dark magic and rule the world." He snorted. "Or whatever."

"If that artifact responds only to the person who holds

it, I think it should've been able to see that you're not gonna go the dark-magic route." He gave her a reassuring smile and nodded. "We both know that."

"Yes." Lily took a deep breath. "With everything people have told us about Optatus witches, it was still kind of an issue in the back of my mind, though, you know? But I don't think that's what the Varelos was talking about. It literally told me there wasn't a difference between hurting people and helping them, so I should've known it wasn't talking about light versus dark magic. I think it was being literal."

"Um...I didn't think there was a difference between using your magic in the day and casting spells at night."

She gave him a playful eye-roll. "There isn't. The Varelos was talking about literal ways of seeing. With light and with darkness. This light—this super-annoying beam I can see all the time." Lily waved her hands in front of her chest and the yellow beam flowed through her hands, which didn't do anything to block out the glow. Romeo's lips twitched. "And I think the darkness is using the Black Heron network. That's literally what it is when I touch the coin. Only nothing before all the grid lines and the weird society-member faces staring at me."

"And the tunnel vision."

"Ha. Yeah. The tunnel vision." She nodded and headed toward the Winnie's side door again. "If I wasn't sure before that this light coming off of me is gonna take me straight to my mom, I'm definitely certain of it now."

"Good." Romeo stepped backward toward the driver's seat and held her gaze. "Then we'll follow it. Weird white shape in the middle of nowhere first, then some gas, then we'll follow the light I can't see."

"Okay."

"Okay."

She smiled at him, turned, and walked down the two steps before she opened the side door and stepped out into the afternoon heat. *Follow the light to Greta Antony. And nothing's gonna stop me.*

TWENTY-NINE

Lily felt so much better about their prospects that her first compulsion spell on the back of the Winnebago almost threw it across the desert. The RV careened forward as if she'd rear-ended it with a bus instead, and Romeo thumped the horn a little louder than she had to get his attention.

"Sorry." Whether or not he could hear her, she shook her head and tried again. "Just because you're figuring things out doesn't mean you have to blast away at everything. Focus. You have more control and much more finesse than that." She released another force blast at the back of the RV, gentler this time, but it still lurched forward. A chuckle escaped her despite how much she wasn't trying to overdo it. "He's gonna start talking about whiplash after this, probably for weeks." She bit her bottom lip, still smiling, and went with an even gentler approach.

Fifteen minutes later, she found the perfect medium

between physical exertion and launching Romeo and the Winnie forward like one of those old rollercoasters that didn't run nearly as smoothly as it should have. It was far easier and much less intense for both of them if she pressed her hands up against the rear fender and pushed a little while she cast a constant stream of her compulsion spell. She thought she was moving them a little faster than he had, which kept her going even after he finally had the chance to steer the Winnie more to the right and toward the strange building in the middle of nowhere.

WHEN SHE HAD BEGUN to feel like she'd reached her limit and needed a break, Romeo opened the driver-side door and shouted, "We're probably good right here."

"Oh. Great." Lily huffed out a sigh, leaned forward against the Winnie a little longer until it rolled to a stop, and straightened. Dusting off her hands, she walked around the side of the RV as Romeo slid out, his plain, dark-green t-shirt pulled over his head. He closed the door behind him and gave her a confused look. "What's wrong?"

"Nothing so far. It's simply not what I expected."

"I guess surprises aren't inherently bad." She wiped her own sheen of sweat off her forehead and smirked. "That's still a good workout, even with magic."

"Yeah, I think you actually moved faster than I did." He nodded. "And I'm not even a little bothered by that."

"It's good to know I don't have to hold back so I won't hurt your feelings."

He snorted. "You wouldn't actually do that, though, would you?"

"Probably not." When she joined him, she widened her eyes and peered around the front of the Winnie. "So what's this unexpected thing that we—oh." She stopped in front of the vehicle and frowned in bemusement.

"Yeah, it's not a building in the middle of nowhere." He shrugged. "That's a tent."

"Wow." The square white tent sat far enough away from the Winnie that they weren't close enough to be considered prying on whoever's personal space included said tent. But there wasn't much out there to hide them, either. "You know, if it had red stripes, I'd wonder where the rest of the circus was."

"Right?" Romeo scratched the side of his head. "Only a tent and nothing else. At all."

"Did you see anyone walking around or anything?"

"Nope. But I know you're gonna say we should still go check it out."

She gave him a sideways glance. "And I know you're gonna agree with me."

He merely gave her a curt nod, and they set off across the dry, barren land toward the tent the size of a single-story, two-bedroom house.

A little wind kicked up toward them and fluttered the sides of the temporary structure and flurried tiny dust clouds. They stopped a few yards away, and Lily cupped her hands around her mouth. "Hello? Is anyone in there?" There was no reply, so she stepped a little closer and tried again. "I'm sorry if we're trespassing. We ran out of gas and hoped someone might be able to help us." The wind kicked up a little more intensely this time, and the sides of the tent rippled with an audible flapping sound.

"If there's no one there," Romeo said slowly and narrowed his eyes at the entrance of the tent, which was pulled down and staked to the ground against the elements, "it's not wrong to go have a quick look inside, right? There might be something we could use—wait. Do you hear that?" He tilted his head and frowned at the ground in front of them.

"Uh...only the wind. I guess that's not what you're talking about."

"It sounds like birds."

"Birds?"

He wrinkled his nose, squinted at the ground again, and nodded. "Yeah. A lot of birds."

A gust of wind picked up behind them again and swirled in a massive cyclone of sand and dust and small rocks. She turned as the funnel settled again and left a dark-skinned man in its place. He wore a loose tunic the color of the desert all around them, loose pants of the same color and soft material, and a wide-brimmed straw hat. A brown mustache and beard fell to the center of his chest, and he folded his arms with a smirk. "You know, most people don't pick up on the birds until much later."

The werewolf startled and whirled, too surprised by the man's sudden appearance to do much more than clench his fists and stare at the stranger with wide eyes. "What... Where did you... How..."

"He blew in with the wind," Lily muttered. "Literally."

The man inclined his head toward them both. "Most people also think they're hallucinating when they find me. Of course, I'm much closer to civilization today, but you never know."

"I'm sorry to show up out of nowhere," she said.

"No, I think he's the one who did that." Romeo looked at her and jerked his thumb toward the man. "And he's wearing a tunic."

"It breathes very well." The man smiled and stepped toward them. "I have a feeling it's a good thing I've stuck around a little longer than usual. I heard someone was coming. Honestly, I thought it would be more grimilkes coming to beg me for eggs again or maybe a few fish. But an Optatus witch and a werewolf. That's definitely a nice surprise. Please, come join me. I'd be more than happy to help if I can." Without waiting for a response, he stepped past them and his pants fluttered behind his legs as a final, much gentler breeze drifted over the sand. He paused at the entrance to the tent, which rolled itself up as if it knew its owner had returned, and he gestured for them to follow. "I think you'll both appreciate this very much. Come on." With that, he vanished into the interior without a backward glance.

"Grimilkes begging for eggs?" Lily glanced at Romeo with wide eyes.

"And fish, maybe." He shrugged. "At least we don't

have to pretend to be something we're not. Or hide what we can do."

"Yeah, and now I really wanna know what's in that tent." Her surprised frown melted away and she grinned. "Let's go."

He puffed out a sigh and followed closely behind her as she headed toward the entrance. She didn't wait for him to catch up before she stepped inside, but she did slow down when a cold tingle washed from her head to her feet the minute she entered. When he came in after her, he sucked in a hissed breath and shivered. "That's oddly refreshing."

The man who'd appeared from the sand and wind stood only a few feet away and smiled at them. The shelter had absolutely nothing else in it. He raised his chin and beckoned them forward. "Only a little more, please." The young couple each took a few small steps forward, and the tent's entrance flap fluttered closed and stretched tightly back into place. "Thank you." Their host stepped back toward the rear wall, the air shimmered, and the tent disappeared to expose a blue sky overhead with only a few clouds. The sand beneath their feet vanished as well, replaced by tall green grasses that rose as high as Lily's knees.

She turned to make sure the tent really was gone, and she found that the desert landscape was too. The same grasses stretched all around them for miles, studded with a few tall trees lush with leaves and even a few budding flowers. When she looked at the man again, he gazed out over the grass in front of them, to where a row of tall reeds rose. By the sound of them, the birds were everywhere, and the smell of the ocean—also a little fishy—filled the air.

"Come," he said. "I have a little overseeing to do, but I would love to speak to you both."

"We really were only trying to find some gas for—" Romeo stopped and looked blankly at Lily when she nudged him in the ribs. "What?"

"I don't think this is the kind of offer we want to refuse right now. Just in case." She raised an eyebrow, and he shut his mouth hastily.

"Okay." He leaned toward her ear and whispered, "Do you know who or what this guy is?"

"Maybe," she said softly. "Let's go find out." She smiled at the man and nodded. "Thank you."

His long beard twitched against his tunic when he smiled and inclined his head. Once the young witch and the werewolf had joined him at the edge of the tall reeds, he pulled a portion of them back like drawing aside a curtain and gestured for them to continue. "Watch the tidepools."

Lily slipped through the opening in the reeds, and Romeo followed her, muttering, "Tidepools. For real?" He glanced at the man and nodded. "Thanks."

On the other side of the reeds stretched a shallow, salt-water inlet, most of it open to the sun but a good deal of it shaded by even more reeds and the tall trees that stretched over parts of the water. The ground sank beneath Lily's feet, and she lifted her foot out of half an inch of water that seeped into her footprint. "Wow."

"It's high tide right now." The stranger nodded and

gazed out over the watery landscape that hadn't existed anywhere remotely close to his tent or the Winnebago. He drew in a deep breath and released it in a satisfied sigh. "Oh. Excuse me. Where are my manners?" Stepping back over the marshy ground, he waved his arms in a big circle and snapped his fingers on both hands. Three Adirondack chairs popped into existence in front of the wall of reeds, followed quickly by a low table, a silver tray, and a steaming teapot with three cups. "Much better. Please. Sit." He pressed his beard against his chest and hiked his pantleg up with the other hand before he sat in the chair behind him. "Why do I never remember to do this for myself?"

"We're sitting?" Romeo muttered.

"Yep." Lily smiled politely and took her seat in the chair between him and the stranger. *Either he's insanely powerful or merely insane. If he can help us, this'll be worth it. As long as it doesn't take too long, of course.*

When she and her companion had both sat, the man straightened a little in his chair and nodded at them. "You may call me John."

Really? All the way out here? "I'm Lily. This is Romeo."

The werewolf merely cleared his throat.

"It's very nice to officially make your acquaintance, Lily and Romeo. Tea?" John gestured toward the ornately painted teapot on the table. When his confused guests took a few seconds too long to answer, he waved dismissively at the whole set. "Or later, perhaps, once you've picked your jaws up out of the marsh." He chuckled, and although it wasn't abnormally loud, a few small brown birds took flight from the reeds behind him.

"We're merely a little...surprised," Lily offered. "Although it's a nice surprise."

"Why, thank you." He nodded in acknowledgment. "It takes a fair amount of upkeep, but I'm quite fond of the way it's turned out."

"Do you...live here?" Romeo asked as his gaze scanned the water and the tall rushes.

"Oh, I suppose. Mostly, I'm simply a wandering spirit looking for something to set my sights on."

The werewolf's eyes grew incredibly wide as he stared at the man seated beside Lily. "You're a ghost?"

"Ha! Please." John leaned back in the chair, slid his forearms along the armrests, and crossed one leg over the other. "There's no room for ghosts out here."

The couple exchanged a glance. *I'm gonna have to wrap this up, I think. Pushing the Winnie back to the road with a few spells will be much faster than whatever we're doing here.* "I'm not trying to be rude—"

"Not at all." Their host gestured airily with one hand, his eyes closed.

"We're kind of in a hurry, actually. Our RV ran out of gas, and we need to get back to the road for a time-sensitive...thing."

"Oh, of course." The man took another deep breath and uncrossed his legs. "It might ease your mind a little if I told you first that time is considerably slower out there. In here...well, we have all the time in the world, really. But I know how eager you are you find your mother, Lily

Antony. She's quite eager for you to arrive as well. Yes." A chuckle escaped him, and she froze.

She didn't have to look at Romeo to know he had fixed his gaze on the man who called himself a wandering spirit. "How do you know all that?" Her voice was barely above a whisper.

"I know far more than I would like, to be perfectly honest." John heaved another sigh. "I will help you, of course. You did find me, after all. But there's something I want you to see first before you're back on your way." Without opening his eyes at all, he raised a hand and pointed out across the water that glistened in the sunlight. "Do you see those funny black birds?"

The young couple turned together and scanned the water. Two large, black-feathered mounds hovered above the water like small umbrellas. One of them shrank and the edges came together toward the center before a small head on a long, thin neck popped up. The bird turned its head to show the profile of a sharp, hooked beak and took a few steps through the shallow water. It crouched and spread its wings again, cupping them around its ducked head to form the umbrella shape once more.

Swallowing, Lily had to try twice before she found her voice. "Romeo?"

"Yeah."

"Just because you were the one who noticed the differ-ence the first time...what kind of bird is that?"

Romeo frowned, scratched the back of his head, and turned to look at her. "I'm taking a guess but I'm fairly sure that's a black heron."

THIRTY

"Very good." John uttered another low chuckle, finally opened his eyes, and straightened in the lawn chair. "I can smell your trepidation, both of you. But tell me, do you know what that clever creature's doing when it curls up like that?" He swung his arms up and around and hunched forward to mimic the same action as the birds. He gave them both a wide grin from the shadow of his curved arms.

"I have no idea," Lily said. *If this is another trick or a trap, we actually walked into it like a couple of idiots.*

"No, I suppose not. It's very clever, really. Very wily and quite sly. Although, of course, one can't blame these birds for those qualities. It's merely in their nature." He laughed again and shook his head. "Be that as it may, the black heron bases its survival, for the most part, on its abilities of deception. It lurks through the water in search of a few fish darting around in the shallows. It ducks its head and curves its wings around itself in that domed shape.

'Why?' you may ask. In the shadow of those hooked wings, the fish who are smart enough to stay hidden under the bright, glistening light of day are stupid enough to believe that the black heron's shadow is, in fact, the sudden onset of night. They think it's safe. They make their move beneath a moonless sky and the black heron sees it all before—" The man darted his hand out toward Lily, his fingers pressed together in the shape of a hooked beak. She jumped, drew in a sharp breath, and released it in a huff when he cackled.

"Yeah, that's freakin' sneaky." Romeo folded his arms and eyed their strange host warily before he glared at the two black herons in their natural habitat.

"Yes. Yes, it is." John nodded and gestured toward the water. "They cannot help themselves. It is what those creatures were born to do, and it is as much learned as it is inherent in their very cores." With a slow tug on his long beard, he turned toward Lily once more and nodded. "The group of wayward magicals who call themselves the Black Heron Society did very well in choosing that name, whether or not they were aware of its connection to these birds, their namesake. But I do not think, Lily Antony, that any of these society members know everything about every black bird, hmm?"

Lily frowned at him and leaned away a little in her chair. "I couldn't begin to guess what they do or don't know."

"Ah, but you already have guessed it, haven't you? That the Black Heron doesn't fully comprehend what you are."

"And you do?"

John nodded slowly and held her gaze. "You are an Optatus. I heard it on the winds and I smelled it on you." He sniggered. "Did you know that the Optatus and the real black herons all stem from the same place? That would be right here, of course." The man pointed at the ground beside his chair and his finger moved up and down as he stared at the young witch.

"In Libya."

"Ha. Well, let's see. Not quite. We are very close to your origins, though. The history of your Optatus blood. There are no permanent rivers in Libya, my dear."

With a frown that evidenced real confusion, she glanced at the water right in front of them, the birds, the reeds, and the overhanging trees. "Then what's this?"

"De Nile." John uttered another wheezing cackle and slapped his knee. "I know that poor joke has been used a few hundred too many times, but I still haven't tired of it."

Romeo leaned forward to stare at the man. "Did you just say we're at the Nile? As in the river?"

"The Nile is most definitely a river, my boy. Oh, was that not your question? Yes, perhaps we are at the Nile. Or a tributary. Some form of it, at any rate, I should say."

Lily interrupted quickly. "The Optatus are from Egypt?"

Their host shrugged, which made his lightweight tunic billow out around his shoulders. "More or less. The current particulars aren't important, Lily. But the past..." He shook his finger at her this time, the digit waving in front of his face as he held her gaze. "The past is quite useful for you. Your mother's captors are only interested in the future. Their future, of course. But the past is not far behind them. Ha! And you are so close now. Do you know why it was so easy for so many Optatus before you to fall into the chains of their own forging?"

The young witch's breath caught in her throat. *Is he feeding Mom's lines back to me?* "Because of how easy it was to get what they wanted."

"Ah. Only for a time. The true reason—the bigger reason and the more fundamental reason—is that their power allowed them to forget. Do not let go of where you come from, Lily. People say, 'Leave the past behind you.' I've never understood why." When John shook his head and gestured over his lap, his beard swung from side to side beneath his chin. "The past is the only thing standing between who you are right now and who you will become after every single decision you make." His eyes widened, and he pressed a finger to his temple as if he'd given her a profound revelation instead of more riddles. "This Black Heron Society has forgotten the past. You can use this to your advantage, my dear. Even now, you are closer to the true black heron than they ever will be." He chuckled. "Figuratively and literally, come to think of it. Isn't that something?"

Lily could only shake her head in bemusement. "I have no idea what that's supposed to mean."

"It means that when you finally reach your mother, take a page out of the old birds' book, eh?" He leaned forward and raised his eyebrows. "Let them think the night has already come."

A breeze rustled through the reeds behind them and stirred up a low, hollow moan. She couldn't tell if it was the sound of it, the coolness of the breeze, or the man's words that sent a shiver up her spine. But she thought she understood what he was saying.

"Okay." Romeo clapped softly and rubbed his hands a little. "Thanks for the great advice, John. We really should... I mean, Lily, we need to get going again, right? Lily?"

"Hmm? Oh. Yeah." She nodded at the strange wandering spirit who might or might not have actually transported them to the Nile for a lesson in magical deception. "Thank you. That's much more helpful than I thought it would be."

"The truth always is." John winked at her and chuckled. "The tea's probably cold anyway." He slapped his hands on his thighs again and pushed himself to his feet. "Come on, then. Just because you haven't wasted any time doesn't mean there's any time to waste." With that, he stepped past the chairs toward the wall of reeds again and swept them aside. This time, though, he stepped through first, leaving them on their own in the sudden oasis they'd stumbled upon.

The young couple shared a glance. Romeo shook his head in disbelief. "I have no idea what just happened."

"That's okay." Lily smiled. "I think I do."

"That was an invitation to follow me, by the way," their host called from the other side of the reeds.

They both pulled aside a section of the tall, waving stalks and stepped through. This time, instead of standing in the tall grasses again, they set foot somewhere else entirely. They weren't in the stranger's tent. They weren't even where they'd left the Winnebago in order to investigate the tent and ask for help. The RV was still there, of course, but now, it stood beside a main road that stretched in either direction in front of them.

"What is going on?" Romeo muttered.

Lily turned again to thank their odd new friend for his help, but both the tent and John were gone. "Wow. I guess being stuck on the side of the road with no gas is better than being stuck in the middle of nowhere with no gas."

"Hey, you know what's even better than both of those options?" When she turned, he held two red, five-gallon gas cans, one in each hand. "Being teleported to the side of the road with enough gas to get us going again." Beside him were seven more cans. "That old ghost actually came through."

Laughing, she shook her head and joined him beside the Winnie. "He wasn't a ghost, Romeo."

"Okay, fine. I'd love to know what he really is, though." He jerked his head up from the gas cans and shook his head hastily. "Actually, I don't. It doesn't matter."

"I guess not." She went to the fuel tank on the side of the vehicle and opened the panel for him. "Here's to only looking at the future. And it's..." She stepped away from the RV to see which way the annoyingly persistent yellow beam was headed. "That way." The line it cut across Libya intersected the road in front of them a little, but they'd follow it off-road again if they had to. She would follow that beam of light anywhere, although the only place she was headed now was that shimmering orange light in the air and the doorway to getting her mom out of the Black Heron's hands.

Romeo lifted the first gas can to the Winnie's tank and poured it in. "We'll fill up and then we'll head out." He studied her far-off expression for a few seconds and tilted his head quizzically. "What did he mean by letting them think the night's already come?"

She turned slowly to look at him and a determined smile spread across her lips. "It means they have no idea what's coming for them."

"You have a plan now, don't you?"

"Yep."

"And I'm really not gonna like it, huh?"

"Definitely not."

He sighed and nodded as the fuel sloshed into the tank. "I thought so."

Lily stepped toward him and ran her hand through his dark curls. "At least you know what you're getting yourself into before we get there."

Romeo let go of the gas can with one hand to pull her toward him. His lips pressed fiercely against hers before he pulled away and grinned. "I knew that the minute you walked through my door after seven years, Lil. Whatever it is, I'm in."

"Good. 'Cause there's really no turning back once we get to the end of that yellow line."

"There never was."

THIRTY-ONE

Greta Antony knelt on the bearskin rug in the center of the High Seat's reliquary and watched the man with the fake eye pace slowly in front of her. She'd overheard the other society members refer to him as Carmichael, but she'd taken to calling him Mikey in the privacy of her own thoughts. The thought of it now made her smirk. For some reason, every time she thought of the name, she imagined a rubber ducky sitting on his left shoulder. Sometimes, it whispered jokes into his ear and other times, it merely squeaked.

If anyone knew any of this, they'd think I'd lost my mind. She watched the man in the smoking jacket move across the room again and again as he turned a hunk of rock in his hand. It was worn smooth with how much he handled it, which might have been a glimpse into his own special form of insanity. *Sometimes, you have to lose your mind to keep it safe. Don't worry, Mikey. You'll never find it.*

"You know what I simply don't understand?" Mikey said and his low voice rang out below the high vaulted ceiling of the reliquary. "That girl is exactly like you, Margaret—stubborn, willful, and infuriating." He stopped his pacing and turned to face her. "So how did she turn out to be so unbelievably stupid?"

She returned his stare, her smirk unwavering even though she swayed a little on her knees. "Feel free to ask her when she gets here."

"Ah. Yes, I'm sure I could. I'm sure she'd give me an answer clever enough to make me doubt what I already know." The smooth hunk of rock turned over and over in his hand. "It won't be enough, though. Not to save you. Not to do what she's coming here to do. I am days away from completing this spell, and once I have your daughter —your blood—standing at my altar, there's nothing you wouldn't give to see her spared. Isn't that right?"

Greta bowed her head and chuckled.

"What's that?"

"I think you have us confused."

"Oh, really?" Mikey tossed the rock in his hand and caught it with a tight little smack. He approached her and squatted in front of her on the bearskin rug. "Do you think your daughter will give me what I need simply to keep me from hurting you more than I already have?" His cold hand settled below her chin and squeezed her lower jaw enough to make her look at him. "Do you think she has it in her?"

Greta gritted her teeth and fought to settle her gaze on his despite how hard it was to focus on any one thing anymore. "I know she does. And she's gonna give you everything she has."

The man clicked his tongue, and his lips twitched away from his teeth in a twisted smile. "That's what I thought." He released her, rose to his feet again, and stepped toward the reliquary doors. Halfway there, he turned again and spread his arms. "She's almost here, Margaret. And we'll welcome her with open arms, won't we?" He raised his eyebrows, spun away, and stormed through the doors. They closed behind him with a loud bang, leaving her alone again in a room with far more comfort and considerably more magic than any in which the Black Heron had held her before.

Greta Antony sat back on her heels and exhaled a long, slow breath. *Lily has it in her, Mikey. More than you could possibly imagine. As long as I'm alive, she'll do what needs to be done.*

Time's running out. Injuries committed to Greta Antony by The Black Heron Society are showing up on her daughter's body. Can she track her mother down before it's too late? Find out in A Witch and A Hard Place.

Get sneak peeks, exclusive giveaways, behind the scenes content, and more.
PLUS you'll be notified of special **one day only fan pricing** on new releases.

Sign up today to get free stories.

CLICK HERE

or visit: https://marthacarr.com/read-free-stories/

For Hire: Teachers for special school in Virginia countryside.

Must be able to handle teenagers with special abilities.

Cannot be afraid to discipline werewolves, wizards, elves and other assorted hormonal teens.

Apply at the School of Necessary Magic.

AVAILABLE AT AMAZON RETAILERS

Halloween has come and gone. I wasn't sure I'd be able to hand out candy this year. One obstacle in the way was how much I ate before the actual night (Reese's are way too delish to resist. A few Almond Joy disappeared as well). The other was the enthusiastic barking from my dogs any time someone approaches the house.

But I came up with a plan. I spent the night sitting in my office near the front of the house binge-watching Jane the Virgin on Netflix. The good dog Lois Lane and the sweet pittie Leela were at the window nearby keeping watch. They were like an early warning system for trick or treaters who were still a block away.

Of course, the system has flaws. Lois has been known to bark just for fun at least a few times every hour.

But, once a tiny Spider Man or a little unicorn was spotted, I grabbed the big bowl of candy, sprinted out of the office, shutting the glass doors behind me and bolted out the front door to meet them on the sidewalk. Happy to say I am still light on my feet.

My neighborhood is fairly new and full of mostly 30-something's and their tiny offspring. Most are still too little to go trick or treating. I wasn't sure just how many little people would be showing up and was surprised at the pretty constant flow.

If the numbers are any indication, I'm going to have to buy candy by the ton in about five years.

There was a Harry Potter and his friend, Ron, and the usual superheroes. Even the parents were dressed up in themed costumes.

My go-to costume as a kid was to be a gypsy. It was convenient that for Christmas every year my little brother and I gave my mom costume jewelry from the local church bazaar. The bigger and brighter the better. Ten months later some of that conveniently became part of my costume. I loved all the shine, glitter and gold.

One snag, which was true for every kid who grew up in the Northeast – (Philadelphia in my case) - and still is. Every costume had to be big enough to fit a winter coat underneath. My arms never went all the way down. It didn't matter. I loved everything about that night. It was like magic had been unleashed, just for one night. There was the neighbor who gave away pennies for every year of our age or the one who gave out full-sized candy bars. Of course, we had the dentist who gave out toothbrushes, but it was still all fun. Even the years it snowed I still hung in there for at least four blocks.

Then there was the annual counting of the candy with

my brother before we touched a single piece. And trading away the sour balls or malt balls for something better, like Three Musketeers. It was one of the few times of the year we had unfettered access to so much sugar as kids.

So much harder to stay away from chocolate as a grown up... But that's a story for another time. More adventures to follow.

Thank you for reading this book, and these *Author Notes*!

Ok, *candy*.

My most memorable moments with a shitake-ton of candy had to do with rain and leaving a brown paper bag of candy out in it.

And bees... Lots and lots of bees.

Back when I was in about first or second grade, we lived in a suburb of Houston, TX with lots of pine trees. We had gone trick-or-treating and had a good haul of the sweet elixir of life. Enough that (I am pretty sure) my mother didn't want us eating it.

Come to think about it as an adult, I wonder if she put that bag of candy BACK out on the swing set so it would get wet?

Nah, I doubt that. *But isn't it strange that I think about this some forty years later?*

Anyway, I searched a day or two later for the candy, to find it outside in the backyard on the swing set, bees buzzing around it. I gathered my courage and made a run for it, the whole swarm of bees trying to protect the nectar of nirvana from the young male stud.

I might have been forty pounds soaking wet.

Maybe.

Anyway, surviving the onslaught of stingers (there were seven total...*maybe*), I retrieved the massive bag of candy, only to find the rain had soaked the candy so bad that even the hard stuff I wouldn't have normally eaten was affected. It was a seriously sad afternoon for me, and it was all thrown away.

I can't stop thinking about whether my mother had really placed that candy out in the rain. I mean, even the hard candy with plastic wrapping was affected. That's...

Just curious.

Hmmm.

I always said when I got older and had money, I'd buy all the candy I want. Unfortunately, I'm older and don't *want* any candy. I think having money is wasted on those of us who are older at times.

However, I eat the hell out of juicy filet mignon steaks —and unlike my younger self, I don't put ketchup on them.

Nor do I eat them well done anymore.

Ad Aeternitatem,

Michael Anderle

OTHER BOOKS BY MARTHA CARR

Series in the Oriceran Universe:

SCHOOL OF NECESSARY MAGIC
SCHOOL OF NECESSARY MAGIC: RAINE
CAMPBELL
ALISON BROWNSTONE
THE DANIEL CODEX SERIES
THE LEIRA CHRONICLES
I FEAR NO EVIL
FEDERAL AGENTS OF MAGIC
THE UNBELIEVABLE MR. BROWNSTONE
REWRITING JUSTICE
THE KACY CHRONICLES
MIDWEST MAGIC CHRONICLES
SOUL STONE MAGE
THE FAIRHAVEN CHRONICLES

Other series:

THE LAST VAMPIRE
THE WITCH NEXT DOOR

OTHER BOOKS BY JUDITH BERENS

OTHER BOOKS BY MARTHA CARR

JOIN THE ORICERAN UNIVERSE FAN GROUP ON FACEBOOK!

BOOKS BY MICHAEL ANDERLE

For a complete list of books by Michael Anderle, please visit

www.lmbpn.com/ma-books/

All LMBPN Audiobooks are Available at Audible.com and iTunes. For a complete list of audiobooks visit:

www.lmbpn.com/audible

CONNECT WITH THE AUTHORS

Martha Carr Social

Website: http://www.marthacarr.com

Facebook: https://www.facebook.com/
groups/MarthaCarrFans/

Michael Anderle Social

Michael Anderle Social
Website:
http://www.lmbpn.com

Email List:
http://lmbpn.com/email/

Facebook Here: https://www.
facebook.com/TheKurtherianGambitBooks/

www.ingramcontent.com/pod-product-compliance
Lightning Source LLC
Chambersburg PA
CBHW050227110726
47898CB00007B/2049